The Cowboy's Simple Solution

Cowboys of Whistle Rock Ranch, Book Eight

Contemporary Western Romance

SHIRLEEN DAVIES

Books Series by Shirleen Davies

<u>Historical Western Romances</u>
Redemption Mountain
MacLarens of Fire Mountain Historical
MacLarens of Boundary Mountain

<u>Romantic Suspense</u>
Eternal Brethren Military Romantic Suspense
Peregrine Bay Romantic Suspense

<u>Contemporary Western Romance</u>
Cowboys of Whistle Rock Ranch
MacLarens of Fire Mountain Contemporary
Macklins of Whiskey Bend

Find all my books at: shirleendavies.com

The best way to stay in touch is to subscribe to my newsletter. Go to my Website *www.shirleendavies.com* and fill in your email and name in the Join My Newsletter boxes. That's it!

Description

She's a widow with a young son and a failing ranch.
He's a ranch hand with a dream and a deep love for one woman.
The only thing missing is a simple solution.

Brady Blackwolf is doing his best to be a top hand at Whistle Rock Ranch. A fast learner and hard worker, he enjoys every aspect of ranching. His days are long and becoming longer. A commitment to a dying friend keeps his off hours busy helping the widow at Kicking Horse Ranch. She sees them as good friends, which forces him to hide his growing feelings for her and her young son.

Amanda Swanson wakes up each morning to the babbling of her young son and the reality of her failing ranch. If Mark hadn't died...but he had, leaving her to achieve their dream alone. She works sixteen hours a day while taking care of her young boy. Still, she is thankful. If Brady didn't help several days a week, the ranch would've been lost long ago. Their friendship, and her son, Marcus, are the bright spots in her life.

Knowing she must make a major change to turn the ranch around, she takes a gamble by partnering with another ranch. Breeding Morgans will either make or break Kicking Horse Ranch. To find success, she must take on a full-time ranch hand.

Brady volunteers. Working side by side, the lines between friendship and something more begin to blur.

Navigating the world of horse breeding, meddling parents, a brush with the law, and an obnoxious neighbor with his sights on Amanda, the two attempt to claw their way to success.

Will the obstacles prove to be more than the couple can overcome, or will they find strength in each other, allowing them an unexpected chance at a future together?

The Cowboy's Simple Solution, book eight in the Cowboys of Whistle Rock Ranch Contemporary Western Romance series, is a clean and wholesome, full-length novel with an HEA and no cliffhanger.

Table of Contents

The Cowboy's Simple Solution

Chapter One

Whistle Rock Ranch, Wyoming
April...

Brady Blackwolf leaned on the corral fence, watching the horses eat their morning hay. He breathed in the crisp morning air, taking a moment to appreciate the beauty of the ranch as he sipped hot coffee.

His cousin, Virgil Redcloud, walked up beside him, coffee mug in hand. "Good morning."

"Morning." Brady nodded, gaze still on the horses.

The two stood in comfortable silence for a few minutes, sipping coffee as the sunlight crept across the valley. From across the way, the sounds of hammering and men shouting drifted down.

Virgil cocked his head. "Sounds like they're making progress on the new cabins. Let's check it out, make sure there's nothing they need from us."

Brady pushed off from the fence. "Right behind you."

The men made their way across the expanse between the corral and rows of cabins. Rounding the first row of cabins, they could see the skeletons of three, two-story cabins taking shape. Today, the construction crew concentrated on the one at the far end. Men were swarming over the roof beams, nailing down braces and joists.

Brady watched them working. "Looking good so far. With luck, the cabins will be ready for guests by late June."

Virgil scratched his chin. "Let's hope so. The Bonners are counting on reservations for the two-story cabins this season."

They watched the construction crew work to finish the roof framing on the cabin. Suddenly, a loud crack had their gazes turning upward. One of the roof braces had split, causing two workers who'd been nailing in joists to lose their footing. They slid down the angled roof, arms flailing as they desperately tried to stop their fall.

"Look out!" Virgil yelled, but it was too late. The two men tumbled over the edge of the roof, falling nearly fifteen feet to the hard ground below. They landed with heavy thuds, crying out in pain.

In an instant, Brady and Virgil were in motion. They sprinted to where the injured men lay groaning, Brady's phone already in his hand as he called 9-1-1.

"It's Brady Blackwolf. There's been an accident at Whistle Rock Ranch. Two men are injured." Pocketing the phone, he knelt down, putting a gentle hand on the shoulder of one worker whose leg was bent at an odd angle.

"Easy there. Help's on the way."

Virgil stood beside the other man, who'd sat up, clutching his arm against his chest. "Looks like you did some damage to that wing of yours."

Despite their injuries, the two men were conscious and cognizant. Without moving them, Brady and Virgil kept them talking, providing comfort until medical help could arrive. Their steady presence brought relief amidst the chaos.

Soon, the sound of sirens pierced the morning air as an ambulance came racing onto the ranch. Barrel, a longtime ranch hand, led two men and a woman toward the fallen men.

The paramedics converged on the scene. Allen, Brady's friend from the volunteer fire department, made a beeline for him.

"What happened here?" Allen asked as he crouched to examine the man's leg.

"The crossbeam up there collapsed," Brady explained, pointing at the partially built cabin. "Sent these two tumbling down."

Allen nodded, deft fingers probing the man's swollen limb. "Compound fracture. We'll need to immobilize him." He swiveled toward the other paramedic. "Jess, get me a splint over here."

Virgil and Brady stepped back to give the paramedics room to work. The men groaned, wincing as the EMTs gently stabilized them, offering each a painkiller, which both accepted. With great care, they used splints to immobilize and align the broken limbs before loading them onto stretchers.

Brady walked alongside Allen as they moved the

men to the ambulance. "Take good care of them."

"You know we will." He closed the ambulance doors.

The ranch hands stood in solemn silence, watching as the ambulance made its way off the ranch and onto the highway.

The activities at Whistle Rock Ranch returned to normal as the ambulance departed, leaving an undercurrent of unease among the ranch hands as they went about their duties.

Brady worked with Virgil and the newly arrived construction foreman to finish securing the construction site. An inspector had been notified, which would stall construction for at least the rest of the day.

Amanda Swanson dragged the manure fork through the soiled straw in the stall, piling the dirty bedding into a wheelbarrow. The rhythmic rasps and clanks of her progress echoed through the cavernous barn. Nearby, her fourteen-month-old toddler, Marcus, gurgled happily in his portable playpen, shaking a plastic set of toy keys.

She paused, leaning on the fork handle as she watched an ambulance race past on the county road leading to the hospital, sirens wailing. She hoped whoever was hurt would be all right. Living out here, help was never close by.

With a sigh, she turned back to her task. The chores weren't going to do themselves, no matter how distracted she got. Following the death of her husband, this place depended on her now. The livestock, buildings, land, and her son were her responsibility. Their future was in her callused hands.

As she mucked, Amanda's thoughts turned to Brady, her neighbor over at Whistle Rock Ranch. She'd seen the ambulance headed in that direction earlier as she'd started work in the barn. Hopefully, he and the rest of those at the ranch were safe.

She'd never admit it aloud, but Amanda admired Brady's dedication to the ranch, and his volunteer work with the local fire department. He was a good man, who spent whatever time he could helping her at Kicking Horse Ranch.

A peal of laughter drew Amanda's attention back to Marcus. To her horror, she realized his playpen was empty. Frantically scanning the barn, she spotted his tiny body standing inside the stall housing a temperamental broodmare.

How had he gotten there without her knowing? she thought, inching toward the stall.

"Marcus," she called in a firm, gentle voice. She didn't want to startle him or the mare.

Watching her son and the mare stare at each other, she cringed when he pointed toward the animal, his face scrunching as more laughter burst forth. He was having a great time while Amanda felt her heart clench.

The stall gate was secure, meaning he'd entered by crawling underneath the lowest metal rung. Unlatching it, she inched the door open. The mare had returned to eating hay in the feeder, giving Amanda the opening she wanted.

She took three steps inside, sweeping him out of harm's way. His delighted giggles faded to whimpers as she left the stall and locked the gate. Holding him against her chest, Amanda exhaled in relief, her heart pounding.

This was the second time in a week he'd managed to escape without her knowing. She needed to find a better way to keep him safe and out of trouble while she worked. It was a problem she'd sort out later, after she calmed down. Right now, she just needed to hold her son. With Mark gone, Marcus was her whole world.

Amanda cradled Marcus in her arms, soothing his whimpers as she carried him back to the playpen. She set him down gently amid his toys, then paused, hands on her hips as she surveyed the flimsy enclosure. This wouldn't do. Not with her active, curious son, who'd learned to climb out of it.

She glanced around the barn, considering her options. The large, empty stall at the end caught her eye. With little effort, it could be converted into a safe play area for Marcus.

Amanda walked to it, looked around, and confirmed her decision. She'd pick up some foam mats and soft toys on her next trip into town, turn it into a cozy spot for playtime.

For now, though, she needed a quick fix. Amanda pushed the playpen against one wall before moving hay bales, stacking them around the other sides to boost the walls. After testing their stability, she stepped back, exhausted but satisfied the bales would hold for the rest of the afternoon.

Marcus grinned at her, already pulling himself up to stand. Amanda shook her head with a wry smile. Her little man was going to be a real handful. She wouldn't have it any other way.

After one more swift peek to ensure Marcus was secure, Amanda picked up the pitchfork and got back to mucking. There were still three more stalls to finish before lunch.

Pausing, she glanced again at her son. His bright eyes and happy babbles filled her heart to overflowing. Amanda smiled, feeling a now familiar sense of awe.

She worked without a break, keeping one ear tuned to Marcus's chatter as she dumped manure into the wheelbarrow. The repetitive motion lulled her into a reflective state, her mind drifting back over the past year.

Losing her husband so suddenly, five months before Marcus was born, had upended her world. There were many dark days when the grief and exhaustion threatened to overwhelm her.

The ranches and community around Brilliance had pulled together, helping keep things running. And Marcus was her ray of light, giving her purpose.

Still, Amanda was aware of how precarious things

were. If something happened to her, what would become of Marcus and the ranch? Her parents had offered to take care of him, giving her time to regroup. They lived across the country in Vermont, and their life was vastly different from the ranch in Wyoming. In the end, she couldn't bear the thought of being separated from her son. This was their home.

An hour later, muscles tight and stomach growling, she set the pitchfork down. Bending, she touched the tips of her boots with the leather gloves worn to protect her hands. Straightening, she scooped Marcus into her arms, heading for the house.

Lunch was a simple sandwich for her and a mixture of canned meat and fruit for her son. As she alternated taking bites of her sandwich and spooning food into her son's mouth, Amanda's thoughts turned toward the future.

She needed to start making contingency plans, just in case. She refused to let fear rule her, not anymore. At the same time, she wouldn't allow herself to be foolish. If anything happened to her, she needed to have her wishes carried out, and not let some court make decisions for her. This ranch was the legacy Mark had built for his family, and she meant to keep it and her son safe.

The last bites of lunch finished, Amanda gathered Marcus in her arms. He played with strands of his mother's hair as they stepped outside. Amanda breathed deeply, loving this time of year. The weather felt warmer than a month earlier, while the air was crisp and invigorating.

Making a decision, she walked back inside to grab her purse and light jackets for both of them. She secured Marcus in his car seat and climbed into the driver's seat of her pickup truck.

As she turned the ignition, her cell phone buzzed with an incoming text. It was from a good friend, inviting her to join a group of local moms for happy hour that evening. Amanda hesitated, torn between her desire for adult conversation and not wanting to disrupt Marcus's routine. And, she mused, there was also the issue of not having anyone to watch her precocious son.

Before heading down the drive, she texted back she couldn't make it, requesting they invite her again in the future. Duty called. She had to pick up feed for the horses, foam mats, and soft toys, then get Marcus home for his bath and bedtime. The same routine, day in and day out.

As Amanda pulled out of the ranch driveway, her phone buzzed again. Glancing down, she saw it was a text from Brady Blackwolf, asking if she could come by to take a look at one of their horses. Virgil and Wyatt Bonner thought the gelding would be excellent for barrel racing, a sport she'd competed in, and now trained horses for buyers.

She typed back to expect her within two hours, after she finished her errands. At least this gave her a purpose for the late afternoon and evening. She often evaluated horses for use in barrel racing and other rodeo events.

Plus, the Bonners paid her to demonstrate barrel racing to guests at their dude ranch. With summer approaching, she didn't want them to forget to call her. Any job working with horses to increase her income was welcome.

Chapter Two

Amanda pulled into the parking area of Whistle Rock Ranch as the sun began its descent into the western sky. She parked next to Brady's white pickup truck, pulled Marcus from his car seat, and headed toward the barn.

Inside, she found Brady grooming one of the horses in the glow of two ceiling-mounted lights. He looked up as she entered, his face somewhat obscured by the brim of his hat.

"Hey, Amanda. Thanks for coming out." Dropping the brush into a tray, he took Marcus from her arms.

"No problem." She rolled up the sleeves of her flannel shirt. "Which one is it?"

Brady gestured to the bay gelding in the crossties. "Apache is three. Bred right here on the ranch. I can saddle him so you'll be able to check him out."

Amanda approached the horse with her usual calm, running her hands down his front right leg and watching his reaction. The gelding didn't flinch. Nor did he react when she picked up each leg to examine knees, ankles, and hooves.

"For a three year old, he's quite calm. He has wonderful conformation. I'd like to ride him."

Brady handed Marcus back to her. "I'll tack up Apache for you."

Ten minutes later, Amanda was in the arena, putting the gelding through what she called her standard testing routine. When finished, she trotted him to the fence, where Brady again held Marcus.

"What do you think?"

She smiled when Marcus reached out for her. "Apache could be a true barrel racing contender. Do you have a buyer?"

"Not yet. Virgil wanted you to check him out. He said if Apache made it through your test, he wanted to hire you to train him. Do you have time?"

Leaning forward, she stroked the gelding's neck. "I'll make time."

"Great. I'll bring him to your place tomorrow morning."

"Make it after eight. I need to set up one of the stalls as a play area for Marcus, and check the one I want to use for Apache."

"Sure thing. I can help you with the play area." Brady tickled the boy's stomach, laughing when Marcus giggled. "Guess you're going to get your own stall. I don't know any other boys who've had the honor."

Amanda let out a breath. "He's climbing out of his playpen. This morning, I found him in the stall with the broodmare. He crawled under the gate. The stall isn't long term. Just until I can hire someone to watch him while I work."

"What about daycare?"

"Same answer. I have to earn enough to afford daycare, whether it's at the house or somewhere else."

"Right."

"Well, I guess I better get Marcus home."

"I planned to come by tomorrow evening to help with those horses you mentioned. Is it all right if I bring Apache over then?"

"Of course. That gives me time to get some other work finished. You can stay for dinner."

"It's a deal."

Amanda drove back to her ranch with a smile lingering on her lips. Having anyone over for dinner had become rare since Mark's death. Brady was a good man, with a wonderful sense of humor.

If she was being honest, she found him quite attractive. Not that she'd ever confess the thought to him. Brady had no shortage of women who'd love to go out with him. Amanda was glad she wasn't one of them.

As she pulled up to the ranch house, she pushed those thoughts aside. She had to focus on Marcus right now. Her son had to be the priority.

After Marcus was tucked into bed, Amanda heated up some leftover chili. She pulled out her laptop and a thick file. The rest of her evening would be spent finishing dinner, drinking coffee, and working on much overdue bookkeeping for the ranch.

Amanda stood in the barn aisle, hands on her hips, surveying the empty stall that would soon be Apache's new home. A hint of a smile played on her lips as she imagined the striking bay gelding's arrival.

The sound of a giggle snapped Amanda back to the present. Whipping around, she spotted Marcus crawling dangerously close to a pile of tools. She swooped him up, eliciting another giggle from the toddler.

"Looks like I've got my work cut out for me," she told Marcus as she deposited him in the makeshift playpen fashioned from an empty stall. It wasn't ideal, but it would do for now.

Satisfied Marcus was secure, Amanda set to work mucking out the stall, thoughts drifting to the afternoon and Brady's arrival with Apache.

The work was soothing, allowing Amanda's mind to wander. She thought of the coming annual spring celebration and wondered what her role would be on the committee. The town looked forward to it all winter, and she found herself proud to be a part of making it an incredible event.

Glancing at her watch, Amanda decided she'd earned a break. After feeding Marcus and taking a quick lunch for herself, she put her son to bed, granting her a couple precious hours to exercise the horses. This work was the reason she stayed. Marcus and the horses.

Later, as she unsaddled the horse, her phone rang, jolting her from her peaceful reverie. Amanda glanced at the caller ID and frowned. She took a deep breath before answering.

"Hi, Mom," she said, unable to keep the weariness from her voice.

Her mother's words came rapid fire in an all too familiar refrain. Why not let her take Marcus for a while? Her parents could fly out and take their grandson back to Vermont. How could Amanda possibly run the ranch alone? Amanda rubbed her temples as she listened. She'd been through this conversation too many times since Marcus's birth.

"I know you're trying to help, but this is my life, Mom," she interjected firmly. "Marcus and this ranch are my future." Marcus's cries from his crib caught her attention.

"I have to go, Mom. We'll talk soon." Amanda ended the call and hurried to comfort her son, disturbed by the conversation. Her parents were wealthy, yet they'd never offered to help her financially since Mark died. They used their money as leverage to force her back to Vermont.

She'd finished changing his diaper when a truck rumbled up the drive. Lifting Marcus into her arms, she stepped out to greet Brady, tamping down her frustration.

"Hey there," Brady called with a wave and an easy grin. "Someone's ready to see his new home."

He nodded toward the trailer holding Apache.

Amanda smiled, her earlier unease vanishing. Together, they led the gelding into his stall. She talked in a calm voice, stroking his neck until backing out of the stall so Brady could secure the latch.

"There you go, boy. Welcome home," she murmured.

Amanda set Marcus down gently in his updated playpen, handing him a stuffed horse to keep him occupied. She watched as he babbled happily to his toy.

"He's getting so big," Brady remarked, leaning on the stall door.

"I know. It's crazy how fast they grow."

With Apache munching on hay and Marcus playing nearby, Amanda brushed a stray wisp of hair from her forehead and exhaled.

"Well, that's one more thing checked off the list. I brought my farrier tools. I'd like to get those two horses shod before supper. What's next for you today?" Brady asked.

Before Amanda could respond, her phone chimed with an updated ringtone. She hurried to answer it, signaling an apology to Brady. He just chuckled.

"Amanda Swanson," she answered.

Brady grabbed his tools. Retrieving a halter and lead line from a hook, he strode to a corral, ready to get to work.

Amanda ended the call and sighed. So much to do and so very little time to accomplish what had to get done.

Brady walked the horse into the barn, noticing the

weariness in her expression. "You all right?"

Amanda forced a smile. "Yeah, I'm fine. That was the Spring Fling Committee chair. We have a meeting tomorrow night at seven in the community hall."

"Works for me. How about I pick you and Marcus up a little before six. We'll stop for pizza or something, then head to the meeting."

"I'd love to eat in town. It's been a while since I've eaten anything I haven't cooked."

"I'm fortunate to be able to eat Beth and Abbie's cooking." Brady looked at the horse he'd brought in from the corral. "I'm going to start with this one and leave the old, mean buckskin for last."

Amanda laughed, then reined in her joy. The buckskin had been Mark's first horse. Now thirty, she wondered how long Old Buck would last.

"I need to get Marcus fed and changed and get dinner going. If you could reshoe those two, I'd really appreciate it."

"You got it."

They parted ways, falling into their respective tasks. Amanda's thoughts churned as she tended to Marcus's needs. She was grateful for Brady's solid presence and willingness to help. But she couldn't rely on him forever. Someday, he'd meet a woman, fall in love, and everything would change. Though she dreaded it, she knew it was another part of life on a ranch.

In the barn, Brady's rhythmic clang punctuated the passage of time. As the sun dipped low on the horizon, they both emerged from their work.

"Dinner's ready when you are."

"I'm ready."

They entered the house, the rich aroma of spicy food filling the air. She'd prepared chicken enchiladas, rice, and black beans, knowing how much he enjoyed Mexican food.

Brady washed his hands at the kitchen sink while Amanda settled Marcus into his highchair. Soon, they were all seated around the table, plates loaded with steaming enchiladas.

"This looks amazing." Brady scooped up a hearty bite.

Amanda smiled, pleased by his response. They took turns feeding Marcus, eating their own food in comfortable silence for several minutes. Marcus's happy gurgles kept them entertained.

"So, what's left to do for the new cabins?" Amanda asked between bites.

He launched into an update, explaining the timeline for completing the additional lodgings. She listened, glad the construction was on schedule after the men were injured.

Their conversation was interrupted by the jangling ring of Amanda's cell phone. She checked the caller ID and sighed.

"It's the town council, probably about the Spring Fling Festival," she explained to Brady before answering.

After a quick call, she looked at him. "They need volunteers to help with planning the children's activities. I said we'd help out."

He nodded. "Happy to, though I know nothing about what would make the children happy."

Amanda chuckled. "Whatever you enjoyed when you were a kid, the same will hold true now."

He chuckled along with her. "Sounds reasonable."

They finished the last bites of their dinner as Marcus banged his spoon happily against his tray.

"I'll clean up while you get him ready for bed," he offered, already gathering up the plates.

"You're a lifesaver." Amanda lifted a sleepy Marcus from his highchair. She changed his diaper and got him into pajamas while Brady tidied up the kitchen. Before long, Marcus was sound asleep in his crib.

She collapsed onto the couch, exhausted and satisfied with the day's accomplishments. Brady joined her with two mugs of coffee and two slices of pie.

"Nothing better than Lydia's boysenberry pie." He handed her a plate.

Lydia had owned Brilliance Coffee & Bakery for several years, adding a second shop in Jackson. Both did a booming business. She did all the baking with the assistance of one helper.

Amanda took a bite and sighed. "So good. And so needed after today."

They ate in tired silence for a few minutes. Despite the long day, she felt good. She didn't know how she would've gotten through life without Brady's friendship.

"The new cabins should be done in about six weeks." Brady updated her between bites. "We can start taking reservations in about a month.”

“That’s great news. After all the time and expense the Bonners have put into the dude ranch, it’s nice to know how successful it’s become.”

Amanda set down her empty coffee mug and turned to Brady. “Thank you for everything today. Bringing Apache over, shoeing the horses, and helping with Marcus. I wish you’d let me pay you.”

Brady shrugged. “No need to pay me. Mark and I were friends. I want to see you and the ranch succeed.”

He held her gaze, his dark eyes full of warmth and sincerity. Standing, he picked up their cups and plates. “I’ll wash these, then drive back home.”

When he set them on the counter, she placed a hand on his arm. “I’ll get these. You’ve done enough. Thanks for everything.”

“If you’re sure?”

“I am. Now, go on and get a good night’s sleep.”

“All right. I’ll see you tomorrow about five-forty-five.”

“We’ll be ready.”

She stood at the open kitchen door, watching as he backed up the truck and trailer, straightened, and headed back the way he came. A pang of longing overtook her, unlike anything she’d felt since Mark died.

Not for Brady, but for all she’d lost when her husband took his last breath. She’d never known a better man, and wondered if Mark would be her one and only. If so, she considered herself blessed.

Chapter Three

Brady's pickup truck rumbled down the rutted drive leading to Amanda's ranch, kicking up a cloud of dust in its wake. He glanced over at the empty passenger seat, imagining Amanda sitting there, her golden brown hair blowing in the breeze from the open window.

Mark and Amanda had been two of his closest friends. Brady hoped he was living up to the promise he made to Mark about watching over Amanda and their child if anything ever happened to him. At the time, Brady didn't think much of it. Almost a year and a half after his friend's death, he thought about the promise all the time.

As he pulled up to the house, Amanda emerged holding Marcus. The toddler's face brightened when he saw Brady, his chubby hands grabbing at the air.

"Well, hey there, partners." Brady stepped from the truck. "Someone looks excited for the big meeting tonight."

Amanda smiled, shifting Marcus to her other hip.

"He's been babbling all morning about 'Bray-dee'. I think he missed his favorite cowboy."

Brady chuckled and took Marcus into his arms. The boy squealed happily, patting Brady's scruffy cheeks.

"I missed you, too, buckaroo," Brady said, tickling Marcus's belly. "Now, let's get loaded up. Don't want to be late."

After securing Marcus in his car seat, they piled into the truck and headed for town. The warm spring breeze drifted through the open windows as Brady and Amanda chatted about the upcoming meeting.

"I'm glad we're on the committee this year," Amanda said. "It'll be nice to give back to the community, especially after everyone was so supportive when..." Her voice trailed off, but Brady knew she meant after her husband's passing.

"Me, too," Brady replied, more to provide support than being excited about the committee work. Except for being a volunteer firefighter, he wasn't much for attending committee meetings. He had heard there'd be a chili cookoff. That, he could get behind.

Amanda nodded, her gaze drifting out the window across the thick forest. Brady studied her profile, admiring her quiet strength. In the time since her husband's death, she'd shown an amazing amount of resilience.

As they neared town, Brady's stomach rumbled loud enough for her to hear.

Amanda laughed. "I guess we better fuel up before the big meeting. I'm starving."

"Now you're speaking my language," Brady said with a grin.

Soon, they were seated in a vinyl booth at the local pizzeria, Marcus happily sipping from a cup filled with orange juice.

Between bites, Brady and Amanda discussed work before switching to sharing their ideas for the Spring Fling. He wanted to help with the chili cookoff, while she thought a petting zoo would be perfect for families.

"It's going to be so much fun," she said, wiping pizza sauce from Marcus's cheeks.

Brady smiled, thinking how much she needed something to keep her mind off the financial troubles of the ranch.

Returning to the truck, Amanda secured Marcus in his car seat before Brady drove the short distance to the community hall.

"Ready for this?" he asked.

Amanda nodded, though her smile seemed a little tense. Brady understood her nervousness. Since her husband's passing, she'd withdrawn from community life to focus on Marcus and the ranch. This meeting marked her reentry into Brilliance's social scene.

Brady gave her arm a reassuring squeeze. "You've got this. And I'll be right there with you."

"Thanks, Brady." Amanda blinked back tears, then straightened her shoulders.

Inside, Brady steered them toward the sign pointing to childcare. "I'll take Marcus and get him settled. You go on and find us a couple seats."

Amanda kissed Marcus's head, handing Brady the diaper bag. Brady tickled the toddler's belly, eliciting happy giggles. "Ready for some fun, little man?"

After dropping off Marcus, Brady entered the main hall. Small clusters of people stood chatting, but he spotted Amanda sitting alone near the front, back ramrod straight.

Sliding into the seat beside her, Brady said, "Got us the best view in the house."

Amanda smiled tightly. Brady surveyed the room. He recognized Laurel Winters, owner of the flower and float store, laughing with Lydia Peralta from Brilliance Coffee & Bakery. Sheriff Duggan stood near the coffee urn, deep in conversation with art shop owner, Daisy Bonner.

Brady raised a hand in greeting as their eyes met. The sheriff nodded in return. "It's good to see some new blood here," Daisy called out with a smile.

"You know it's gonna be a party with us on the job," Brady replied, winking at Amanda.

She glanced around the room, taking in the familiar faces. Her gaze landed on Laurel, seated a few rows ahead. Laurel had been on the Halloween Festival committee the year before Marcus was born. Amanda remembered hearing about Laurel's boundless energy and gift for bringing people together.

Making a decision, Amanda stood and walked over to Laurel. "Mind if I join you?" she asked.

Laurel's face lit up. "Amanda. Of course, have a seat." She patted the chair next to her.

Amanda slid into it with a sigh. "It's so nice to see

you again. I wanted to pick your brain about the festival. You always made everything look so effortless."

Laurel waved her hand. "Oh, it was far from effortless. But it was rewarding." She leaned in conspiratorially. "The secret is getting the right people in the right roles. Play to everyone's strengths."

Amanda nodded, soaking up Laurel's wisdom. Before she could reply, the mayor called the meeting to order.

"Welcome, Spring Fling Committee!" Jupiter Jones's voice boomed across the room. "We've got a lot to cover tonight, so let's get started..."

He dove into an overview of the festival timeline and budget. Amanda's head swam trying to keep up. She shot an anxious glance at Brady down the row from her, who gave her a subtle thumbs up.

The mayor clicked to the next slide, which displayed the festival site map. "Now, as you can see, we'll have three stages, over a hundred vendors..."

Amanda stifled a groan, settling in for a long meeting.

She tried to focus as the mayor droned on about the various elements of the festival, but her mind kept wandering. She thought about Apache and the training session planned for the next morning. When the mayor mentioned the chili cookoff, she recalled Nacho's award-winning chili verde. Maybe she could convince him to whip up a batch.

She was jolted back to attention when the mayor

mentioned the next topic. "So, for the children's area. I understand Amanda Swanson and Brady Blackwolf will chair that committee. They'll need volunteers to run the games, face painting, balloon animals. You know. Make it fun for the little ones."

Laurel elbowed Amanda lightly. "I'll help you and Brady out. I can probably get Aiden to help, too," she whispered. "Oh, and I'm certain Lily Redcloud will want to be involved."

"Any help is welcome. Thank you."

As the meeting progressed, she felt her excitement growing. The only downside was the committee meetings, except for one, would be virtual going forward. She'd miss the camaraderie and spontaneous conversations of meeting in person.

After ninety minutes, the mayor adjourned the meeting. There was a clear plan and assignments for all. Amanda stretched and stood up, exchanging a grin with Brady.

"Well, that wasn't so bad," he said. "I'm glad Aiden showed up. He's going to work on the chili cookoff committee with me and a few others."

"Sounds perfect. I'm impressed with the way Jupiter ran the meeting." Amanda was already thinking about ideas for games and crafts. She couldn't wait to see the kids' smiling faces at the festival.

Brady drove Amanda back to her ranch. It was close to nine at night, and Marcus was sound asleep in his car seat. He knew she must be exhausted after the long day, between working the ranch and attending the committee meeting.

"So, do you have any ideas yet for the kids' area?" He glanced over at her in the passenger seat.

"Tons. I was thinking we could do a ring toss, face painting, temporary tattoos..." She trailed off, her mind spinning with possibilities.

Brady chuckled. "Well, don't go planning the whole thing without me now. Just because I'm helping with the cookoff doesn't mean I won't be available to work with you, right?"

"You're right. I'm just excited. I definitely want to hear your ideas."

As they pulled up to her ranch, he turned to Amanda.

"Thanks for getting me involved. I'm not someone who volunteers much."

Her eyes softened. "I should be thanking you. To be honest, I'm not certain I would've gone forward with this without you. It would've been easy to stay home."

Brady understood. Getting out of the truck, he carried a sleeping Marcus inside and tucked him into his crib while a tired Amanda looked on.

"Well, I guess I'll head out and let you get some rest," Brady said. "I'll be by tomorrow afternoon to help with the hay delivery."

"That sounds good. See you tomorrow, Brady. And thanks again." She closed the door behind him, grateful for his friendship and support.

Amanda woke at sunrise, feeling rested and energized about the day ahead. After getting dressed, she peeked in on Marcus, who was playing with a stuffed horse Brady had given him. She quietly closed the door before walking down the hall to the kitchen.

Preparing coffee and toast for herself and cereal for Marcus, she returned to his bedroom. Babbling while she changed and dressed him, they ate, then headed to the stables to start prepping Apache for their training session. Surprising her, Marcus pointed toward his stall. Setting him down, he beelined for the box of toys, forgetting all about his mother. She turned on the monitor, checking to make certain her phone had made the connection before closing and latching the gate.

The crisp morning air filled her lungs as she stepped outside the barn to look around. She inhaled, taking in the familiar smells of hay and horses.

Turning around, she entered Apache's stall and began brushing the handsome bay gelding, murmuring words of encouragement. The horse nickered in response.

Once Apache was tacked up, she checked on Marcus, then led the horse into the corral behind the barn. She started with light warm-up work, and as the minutes ticked by, she worked with the gelding on sidepassing.

The rumble of an engine broke the stillness of the morning. Amanda turned to see a shiny black sports car pulling up the drive. Her gaze narrowed as she watched the driver, a tall man in expensive clothing stepped out and approached her.

"Excuse me, miss," he called out. "I seem to be a bit lost. Could you point me toward the interstate?"

She gave him quick directions, annoyed by his brusque tone. The man gave a curt nod, clearly in a hurry. Without even a thank you, he got back in his car and sped off, leaving a trail of dust in his wake.

Shaking her head, she focused on Apache. She wouldn't let the rude interruption ruin her morning. Taking a deep breath, she gathered the reins and prepared to try the sidepass again.

Clicking her tongue, she urged Apache into a walk around the perimeter of the corral. As they rounded the first corner, she applied gentle pressure with her legs, asking the horse to sidestep away from the fence. Apache hesitated, then took a few clumsy steps sideways before stopping.

"Good try, buddy." She patted his neck, deciding to break the maneuver down further. Sitting deep in the saddle, she flexed her right leg against Apache's side while pulling the reins slightly to the left. The cue was subtle but firm.

At first, Apache only turned his head, but Amanda held the aids steady. After a moment, the horse shifted his weight back and crossed his right front and hind leg over, sidepassing for several smooth strides.

"Yes!" Amanda exclaimed, releasing the cues and praising Apache. They continued for a bit before trying the other direction with equal success.

Sliding to the ground, she patted his neck, whispering praise before leading him back into the barn.

Chapter Four

Amanda wiped the sweat from her brow as she hauled the last bale of hay into the barn. She paused to catch her breath, looking out over the expanse of Kicking Horse Ranch. The place was barely holding together, just like her.

Ever since losing her husband, she'd struggled to keep the ranch afloat on her own. Between caring for Marcus and trying to run the ranch solo, she was spread much too thin. She needed help and, until now, was too stubborn to ask.

After Marcus settled down for his nap, she called Brady. The ranch hand had become a good friend, and she trusted his judgment.

"Hey, Brady, it's Amanda. I know it's a lot to ask, but do you think Wyatt Bonner might have some time to talk with me? I could really use his advice on how to get this place on solid footing."

Brady thought it a good idea and offered to set up a meeting. The next day, Amanda pulled up to the sprawling Whistle Rock Ranch. Though nervous, she steeled her resolve. Swallowing her pride, she walked into Wyatt's office.

His features creased into a sincere smile. "Amanda. Good to see you. Have a seat and tell me what's on your mind."

She settled into the leather chair across from him. "I appreciate you taking the time to meet with me. I know your family has already done so much, paying off the mortgage and carrying the paper..."

He waved his hand. "We look after our neighbors around here. Pop and the rest of us believe if our neighbors do well, we'll do well. Now, tell me, what can I do to help you?"

Amanda took a deep breath. "I need to make the ranch profitable again. With just me running it, we're drowning. I thought maybe I could start breeding horses."

He drummed his fingers on his desk as he considered her idea. "Breeding can be a solid business, but it takes some investment up front and a good bit of time to become profitable."

Shoulders slumping, she stared down at her worn boots.

"But," Wyatt continued, "with some creativity and grit, there's potential in your idea."

Amanda looked back up, a glimmer of hope in her eyes. "I'm willing to do whatever it takes."

A knock at the door stopped the rest of her reply. "Come in," Wyatt called out.

The door swung open, and Virgil Redcloud strode in. "Sorry, I'm late. What did I miss?"

Wyatt gestured to the empty chair before explaining her reason for the visit. "Pull up a seat. We were just getting started."

Virgil settled into the chair beside Amanda. His keen eyes studied her. "So, what ideas have you got so far for making Kicking Horse profitable?"

Amanda met his gaze. "I was thinking about starting a breeding program. Mark had a lot of knowledge about the best lines to breed. Me, well, not so much."

Virgil rubbed his chin thoughtfully. "If you had your pick, what horse breeds would you pick?"

"Quarter Horses, as I understand them better than other breeds," she admitted. "Since you folks have one of the premier Quarter Horse breeding programs in the country, I'd love your input on what other breeds to consider."

The two men leaned forward, launching into a lively discussion of horse breeds, investment of time and money, and demand. She listened, chiming in with the occasional question. Her mind whirred with new possibilities, from Paints to Morgans to Quarter Horses.

This was the guidance she required. She nodded as Virgil explained the nuances of breeding quality cow horses. Wyatt's office door swung open, and Anson Bonner strode in. The patriarch of the Bonner clan had a commanding presence. His keen eyes swept over the gathering.

"Well, now, what do we have here?"

Wyatt stood to greet his father. "Pop, you remember Amanda Swanson. We're just having a chat about the future of her ranch."

Anson clasped her hand. "Of course. I'm pleased to see you, my dear."

He settled into a vacant chair and fixed her with an intent look while Wyatt explained the reason for her visit.

Anson leaned back in his chair. "If you're aiming to establish a quality breeding program, a partnership with Whistle Rock could benefit you." He looked at Wyatt. "It could benefit all of us."

Her eyes widened. A collaboration with the prosperous Bonner ranch could be a game changer.

Anson thought a moment before providing more details. "Our Paint and Quarter Horse breeding operations are among the finest in the country. However, I've been considering the introduction of Morgans or perhaps Appaloosas. I have connections who could line us up with top-notch stallions and mares to establish our own bloodlines in either breed."

"What do you think, Amanda?" Wyatt asked.

"Well, it hadn't occurred to me a partnership might be possible. It could be an ideal situation for my ranch. Linking with Whistle Rock would have immediate name identification."

"What about a specific breed?" Virgil asked.

She thought for a moment. "I have a fondness for Morgans and more experience with them than Appaloosas. Morgans are easy to train, have an even temperament, and a real affinity for their owner."

"They are friendly." Anson chuckled.

Amanda smiled. "Yes, they are. They also make excellent trail horses."

Her mind reeled, even as a spark of excitement flared inside her. A partnership with Whistle Rock would be a lifeline for Kicking Horse. But it also meant deeper dependence on the Bonners. Could she swallow her pride and accept their help?

A collaboration could be precisely what Kicking Horse needed to thrive. Whistle Rock's expertise with its elite Paint and Quarter Horse breeding programs would be invaluable.

She carefully chose her next words: "I'm grateful for your generous offer. Becoming partners would provide resources I simply don't have right now." She met each man's gaze. "Could I have a few days to think through this?"

Wyatt nodded. "Of course. We need some time, also. My brothers, Jonah and Gage, would be involved, as we'd want their opinions. This doesn't need to be decided today."

Virgil leaned forward, his voice earnest. "Whatever you decide, we're here to help however we can. Kicking Horse has always been like family."

Anson nodded in agreement, his craggy features softening into an encouraging smile.

Overwhelmed by their support, she felt her reservations begin to thaw. Perhaps this was not charity, but community.

"Thank you," she said, her voice thick with emotion. "I can't tell you how much this means."

Amanda's mind buzzed as she drove to town to pick up Marcus from the church's daycare program. The meeting with Wyatt, Virgil, and Anson had given her much to think about. A partnership with Whistle Rock would provide resources she desperately needed—expertise, contacts, financial backing. It also meant sacrificing some control.

She needed time to consider all her options. Rushing into the wrong decision could ruin everything she and Mark had worked toward.

She felt the weight of responsibility settling on her shoulders once more. Kicking Horse Ranch meant a great deal to her. It had become her home and her son's legacy.

Picking up Marcus, she secured him in his car seat before turning toward home. She replayed the conversation with the three men, considering, once again, all the possibilities they'd discussed.

If only Mark had lived. He'd know what to do, the questions to ask, and what to avoid.

The ranch had been improving over the last months before his death, all because of his experience.

"I miss you so much," she murmured, swiping at a tear rolling down her cheek.

Throat tight, she turned the truck off the main road onto the driveway leading up to the ranch house. She was tired of doing everything alone. Except for the precious few hours when Brady was around, her life had become one of solitude. She wondered if Marcus hadn't been born, would she have already given up and moved back to Vermont as her parents wanted?

To her eternal joy, Marcus had been born. Her heart surged with love and purpose. She would find a way to make this work, even if it meant compromises. Her son deserved a full, happy childhood on these beautiful acres.

As the ranch house came into view, Amanda saw Brady exercising one of the horses in the round pen. He gave a quick wave when spotting her truck.

Parking, she scooped up Marcus, breathing in his sweet baby scent as her mind churned with possibilities. She needed to have a serious talk with Brady about the Bonners' offer to partner on breeding programs. There were pros and cons to consider, and he had a way of simplifying complex ideas.

The Bonners' help would be a huge help in making the ranch profitable again. Expanding into breeding could provide a steady income stream. Plus, having access to Whistle Rock's premier training facilities would be invaluable.

Heading into the house, she set Marcus down for his afternoon nap. She wished Mark were here to weigh in. He'd always been the levelheaded one, balancing her passionate spirit with practical wisdom.

A soft knock at the door pulled Amanda from her

thoughts. She opened it to find Brady holding a large bundle of firewood.

"Where do you want me to put this?"

"The box next to the fireplace would be great. Thank you." Even with the change from winter to spring, the evenings and early mornings were chilly.

As he stacked the wood, she made a snap decision. She'd ask him to stay for dinner and share what had transpired during the meeting. His insights could prove invaluable.

Amanda poured two mugs of hot coffee and headed out to the living room, where Brady entertained Marcus after dinner. Setting the mugs down, she lifted her son up into the air before settling him on one hip.

"I'll put him to bed. Do you have some time to stay and talk?"

"All the time you need." He picked up a mug, taking a sip as she headed down the hall.

Returning, she cradled the mug in her hands, gathering her thoughts. "I wanted to get your opinion on something. I met with the Bonners today about ways to improve the ranch."

He leaned his back against the hearth, feeling the heat from the fire as he stretched out his legs. "I heard. How'd it go?"

"Mr. Bonner proposed a partnership between my ranch and Whistle Rock, focusing on a joint horse breeding program."

"Anson?" The rise in his voice conveyed his surprise.

"Surprised me, too." She went on to outline the main points of Anson's suggestion, watching for a reaction from Brady, spotting no telltale signs of what he thought. When finished, she took another sip from the mug, her eyes fastened on his.

"It's a generous offer, Amanda."

She sighed. "I know. More generous than I ever expected."

"What are you worried about?"

"Losing control. It was one of the issues Mark always brought up when we discussed the ranch's future. With a partnership, there's the chance the Bonners will end up running Kicking Horse instead of me."

He stared at her for a long while, lost in thought. When he spoke, it was with the clarity she hoped to hear.

"Set up the partnership so you have a fifty percent vote. They're providing the funds, you're supplying the manpower. Fifty-fifty. The risks are spread out between both ranches. What will happen if you don't go forward?"

"The odds are, I could lose the ranch to the Bonners."

He nodded. "Given the way you're already headed, in my mind, it's not much of a choice. Virgil and I have talked a lot about the Bonners and Whistle Rock Ranch since I arrived. The two unwavering factors are the family's honesty and integrity. The other factor to consider is how almost everything they start is a success. Truthfully, I haven't heard of any failed ventures. If I were to partner with anyone, it would be the Bonners."

Chapter Five

Amanda strode into Wyatt's office, a stack of papers tucked under her arm. Her pace slowed as she approached the large desk where Wyatt, Virgil, and Jonah were already gathered.

"Sorry I'm late," she said, taking the empty seat next to Virgil. "It took more time dropping Marcus off at the church than I'd planned."

Wyatt gave her an easy smile. "No problem. Does everyone have a copy of the agreement?" When they nodded, he looked at Amanda. "I know we've gone over the details on the phone, but I want to go through them once more to make sure everything is clear. I'll start by summarizing the key benefits of this partnership."

He slid a folder toward him, pulling out a copy of the agreement, as well as another piece of paper with numbered notes. Wyatt began enumerating the benefits from Whistle Rock Ranch's point of view, slowing when he reached the end of the list.

"Finally, I believe with our shared resources and

expertise, both ranches stand to see some substantial profits once the program has a stable of trained Morgans," Wyatt finished. "Keep in mind, this isn't expected for at least three years."

Virgil looked at Amanda. "Mark did a good job laying out Kicking Horse for breeding purposes. It saves us a great deal of time and money to use what you have in place."

She gave a slow nod. "My main priority is making sure the ranch prospers. This has been a tough couple of years since Mark's death. I do believe this partnership is the right move. I do have a question about section 3B," she said. "It's not very specific. I'd like more detail."

Jonah cleared his throat, shifting to face Amanda. "I can understand your desire for more clarity there," he said. "As the one who drafted this agreement, let me explain the thought process."

He described the income and payout structure, pointing out how various factors would determine the percentages each entity would receive.

"The intent of this provision is to allow you to earn a living wage while the breeding program takes hold. As Wyatt said, it will take a while to generate a profit from our efforts. In the meantime, you have to make enough to support yourself and Marcus."

"Thanks, Jonah. I appreciate you including this, but I don't want to be paid if I haven't contributed to the partnership."

"You're going to be doing a lot to contribute, Amanda," Wyatt said. "Your part will be more intensive in the short term. Once we have some stock to train, then we'll be putting in more time to market and sell the horses. It will all balance out."

"If you're sure, then I'm fine with the structure." Sitting back, she forced herself to relax. The decisions she made now would affect her and Marcus for a long time.

"All right, let's go through the rest of the agreement so Jonah can answer any other questions you have," Wyatt said. "We don't want you to sign anything until you're one hundred percent certain this is satisfactory for you."

"You're also encouraged to have your own attorney go through this," Jonah said.

She smiled at him. "Well, since I don't have an attorney, you'll just have to put up with my questions."

"Not a problem, Amanda."

Over the next hour, Amanda, Wyatt, Virgil, and Jonah discussed the rest of the agreement in detail, making minor revisions. Though tense at times, the conversation remained professional and productive. It was clear everyone shared the goal of creating a solid foundation for the partnership.

With all the sticking points resolved, Jonah printed a final copy of the agreement for everyone to sign. Amanda took a deep breath and picked up the pen, feeling a swell of anticipation, uncertainty, and hope as she scribbled her signature.

The others followed suit, solidifying their commitment. As they shook hands, Amanda felt a sense of excitement about the future. This partnership represented a bold new chapter for Kicking Horse Ranch.

Amanda took a deep breath as she stepped outside the lodge, the signed agreement in hand. Though she felt excited about the possibilities ahead, a part of her was still anxious about all the unknowns.

Walking to her truck, she saw Virgil and Brady loading up equipment, preparing for the trip to Kicking Horse Ranch the following morning.

Amanda waved. "See you guys in the morning."

Virgil tipped his hat in reply. "We'll be there bright and early to unload."

Amanda nodded, climbing into her truck. Starting the engine, she found herself already making mental lists of everything she needed to prepare. There was so much to do before the Whistle Rock team arrived.

The next morning, Amanda was up before dawn, dressing and feeding Marcus before tidying up the barn. She wanted everything to look its best when Wyatt, Virgil, and Brady arrived. As she worked, Amanda thought about how much she'd already learned from the experienced ranchers.

Right on time, she saw a truck coming toward the barn. She shielded her eyes against the morning sun and made out Wyatt behind the wheel, with Virgil riding shotgun and Brady in the back seat.

Gathering Marcus, she walked out to greet them with a smile. "Morning, gentlemen. Thanks for coming out."

"Happy to be here," Wyatt replied.

"Let's take a look around and see what needs to be done before we unload the equipment," Virgil added.

Amanda nodded, gesturing for them to follow her.

She led Wyatt, Virgil, and Brady into the larger of two barns. Their first visit had given them a broad overview of the ranch and its layout. This visit was meant to delve into specific items requiring attention.

As they walked, she moved Marcus to her other hip, pointing out areas she believed needed improvement. They'd been standing outside the large barn when an almost new pickup truck approached, parking near the group.

Dr. Dorrie Worrel stepped out, wearing her signature cowboy boots and a faded denim shirt. "Hope I didn't hold anything up," she called out. "There was a difficult birth at the Miller ranch this morning. The foal made it, thank goodness."

Amanda smiled and shook the veterinarian's hand. "We're glad you could make it. I really appreciate you taking the time."

"Happy to help any way I can," Dorrie replied. She turned her keen eyes toward the barn.

Amanda felt a prickle of anxiety as the veterinarian scrutinized her facilities. She wanted to make a good impression on the seasoned ranchers and prove she was serious about the partnership.

"Amanda, we're going to unload the equipment while you talk with the doc," Brady said.

"Thanks." She turned toward Dorrie, setting Marcus on the ground and taking his hand. "Why don't we take a look inside?" Amanda suggested, leading her into the larger barn, the one used for birthing. She slid open the wooden doors, sunlight streaming into the dim interior.

Dorrie stepped inside, slowly walking the aisle between the stalls. Amanda trailed behind, interested to hear the woman's suggestions.

After several minutes of observation, she turned to face Amanda. "Ventilation needs some improvement," she remarked. "And the lighting could be brighter. The birthing stalls are excellent. I might suggest modifications after a few births take place."

She made mental notes as Dorrie continued, explaining proper drainage, and options for fans and skylights. She listened, asking questions based on her limited experience.

After examining the other structures, Dorrie concluded with some recommendations for safer fencing. She shook the doctor's hand again. "Thank you, this has been incredibly helpful."

Lifting Marcus into her arms, she walked Dorrie back to her truck, feeling a rush of relief and renewed excitement. Mark had done a remarkable job preparing the ranch for breeding. She wished he was still with her to hear all the compliments on his hard work.

Two hours later, Amanda watched Wyatt, Virgil,

and Brady walk to their truck. This meeting marked an important milestone, the official start of a partnership between the ranches.

Turning to Wyatt, Amanda extended her hand. "I can't thank you enough for all your work to make this happen."

He grinned, shaking her hand. "I'm happy we could work out an arrangement that benefits everyone."

She then faced Brady and Virgil. "Thank you both for being so generous with your time, knowledge, and resources. I'm truly grateful for your guidance, and I look forward to learning more as this partnership progresses."

"We're excited to work together," Virgil replied. "I have a feeling this will be the start of a very successful collaboration. We'll make sure you and Kicking Horse get everything you need to build up a top-notch breeding and training program."

As the truck pulled away down the drive, Amanda gave Marcus a squeeze.

"This is all for you, my sweet boy," she whispered. "For our future." She stood on the porch, watching the truck fade from view, filled with anticipation for the work ahead.

The following morning, holding Marcus by the hand,

Amanda took a deep breath as she looked out over the pastures of Kicking Horse Ranch. She imagined the now empty fields dotted with sleek, muscular Morgans, grazing with their foals, yearlings testing their speed in play.

She knew it would take years of diligent work, but the breeding program with Whistle Rock Ranch would be in place within months. Foals would be born the following spring, while she honed her training skills on older horses. Amanda felt immense pride in what they would be able to accomplish.

In the distance, she spotted an approaching truck, recognizing it as Brady's. She hadn't expected him this morning. Parking not far from her, he climbed out.

"Good morning, Brady."

"Morning. I was on my way to pick up supplies and wanted you to hear the good news. Any chance you have coffee?"

"Sure do. Come on inside, and you can tell me about this good news."

Entering the kitchen, she handed Marcus to Brady before pouring two cups of coffee. Sitting at the kitchen table, she looked at him.

"All right. Tell me what you know."

"Anson received several responses from his contacts about available Morgan studs and mares. He and Wyatt are flying out this afternoon to look at them. If all goes well, there's a good chance you'll have breeding stock arriving within a week or two."

"One to two weeks? Do you think I'm ready?"

He reached out, placing his hand over hers. "Amanda, you're as ready as you'll ever be. Remember, whatever happens, Whistle Rock will go through each step with you. And, hey, you've got me to help you out. It's real simple."

Chapter Six

Amanda stood on the front porch of the ranch house, holding a frosty glass of lemonade in her hand. Her body twisted as she moved the glass several times to keep it away from an annoyingly persistent bee.

She reluctantly considered giving up and going inside when an unfamiliar car approached on the long drive to the house. Squinting, she tried to make out the occupants through the glare on the windshield. As the car pulled to a stop, her eyes widened in surprise.

"Mom? Dad?" Amanda gasped as Peggy and Reginald Aldrich stepped out of the car. Setting down her glass, she almost tripped on the steps in her haste to reach them. "What on earth are you doing here?"

Peggy rushed forward to embrace her daughter. "Surprise! We wanted to come see our darling girl and grandson."

Reginald gave Amanda a quick hug. "It's been too long, Amanda. I didn't remember this place being so, well...rustic." His gaze swept over the worn ranch buildings and equipment.

Ignoring the barb, Amanda led them inside, where Marcus played on the floor. Peggy rushed to him, scooping the toddler into her arms while cooing next to his ear.

"I hope you don't mind us dropping in unexpectedly," Peggy said, settling on the couch with Marcus. "We were nearby and thought we'd stay for a few days. Maybe a week, if you don't mind."

What was she to say? They were her parents, after all. "Of course I don't mind. Have you eaten?"

"We stopped for lunch in town. Linda's Diner, right, Peggy?" He looked at his wife.

"Very quaint. The food was better than either of us expected." She bounced Marcus in her lap, unaware of the boy's growing agitation.

"Here. Why don't I take him for a bit, Mom." Marcus all but launched himself into his mother's arms. "He can be a real handful after a few minutes. So, did you come out to visit friends?"

"You know your father. Reggie got a wild idea we should visit South Dakota, see Mt. Rushmore and the monument to that Indian leader."

"Crazy Horse Memorial, dear," Reggie said. "Very impressive."

"Yes, I've seen it, Dad. Mark drove us up there on one of our few vacations." A whisp of melancholy entered her voice. "Anyway, I'm glad you two were able to see the memorials. They're in a beautiful part of the country."

"Well." Her father pushed himself out of the chair.

"I should bring in our bags."

"Do you need help?" Amanda asked.

"I can get them. You can show me where we'll sleep."

When she tried to put Marcus down, he whimpered, refusing to let go of her. She'd never seen him act this way before. "All right, little man. You can come with me. Your bedroom is down the hall on the right, Dad."

Reggie followed her, taking in the space about one-tenth the size of their bedroom in Vermont.

"The guest bath is across the hall, Dad."

"Ah...yes." She didn't see how his nose crinkled at the tiny bath. "Very good. I'll be right back."

Watching him walk back down the hall, she let out a shaky breath. The last time both parents had visited was for three days to attend Mark's funeral. They hadn't come by the ranch, preferring to stay in a bed and breakfast in town.

Her mother had flown out when Marcus was born, planning to stay three weeks. She'd left after ten days, which Amanda thought was seven days too long. With everything going on, she had no choice but to continue with her schedule. She hoped her parents understood. If they didn't, this could be another very short visit.

Over the next two days, Amanda continued with her planned activities, even leaving for a meeting at Whistle Rock Ranch. So far, her parents had kept their disapproval of her lifestyle well hidden. Her father had even volunteered to help her with morning and evening chores. Reggie grimaced at cleaning animal pens, and the manual labor required to run the ranch, but didn't complain.

Her mother had more trouble hiding her disapproval. Peggy pursed her lips at the simple home-cooked meals Amanda prepared.

Finally, on the third evening, their true feelings came to the surface when Brady came by to help exercise horses and work in the birthing barn. Her father had shaken his hand, then returned to the house. Peggy had ignored him until he walked inside with Amanda for dinner.

"I can smell the wonderful aroma of your enchiladas," he said as they entered the kitchen, holding Marcus in one arm. "Am I right?"

"You are. I've also prepared rice and beans and will warm the extra tortillas now." Amanda's smile faded when she spotted her mother at the kitchen table, a stony look on her aristocratic face. "I don't believe you've met my mother, Brady."

"Not yet." He smiled, receiving a cold stare in return.

"Mom, this is Brady Blackwolf. He's been a huge help around here since Mark's death. Brady, my mother, Peg—"

Her mother stood suddenly, interrupting the introduction. "Mrs. Aldrich." She didn't extend her hand or offer anything more before leaving the kitchen.

Amanda stared after her, embarrassed at her mother's behavior. She turned to look at Brady, shaking her head. "I'm sorry."

"Hey, I've been treated better and worse. Not a problem." The smile he sent her didn't show the usual warmth. "Maybe I should take off."

"Not a chance, Brady. I made the enchiladas for you, not them. If they don't like it, they can go out for dinner."

Which is what they did.

Her parents broached the subject which brought them to Brilliance, five days after arriving, as the three adults sat on the porch watching the sunset.

"Amanda, your father and I are concerned," Peggy began gently. "Are you sure this is the best environment to raise Marcus? The work here seems awfully strenuous for a young widow."

Her father chimed in. "Why not sell this place and come back east with us? Marcus would have every opportunity back home. You could take it easy while we help with the boy."

Amanda stiffened, gripping the arms of her chair, forcing herself to stay calm. "This ranch is my home now. Mark and I dreamed of raising our family here. I can't give up on the dream we shared."

Peggy pursed her lips. "But is it safe? Surely, Marcus would be better off in civilization."

She chuckled. "This is civilization, Mom. Marcus needs wide open spaces to run free, not staid country clubs. I won't have him growing up believing he's entitled and ignorant of hard work."

"Now see here, young lady," Reginald said, leaning forward in his chair. "You should be thankful for all we've provided you. Marcus deserves more than a few head of cattle and calloused hands."

Amanda's fists clenched at her sides. "I am thankful. Please don't think I'm not. You need to understand this is my life now, which means it's my son's life. I've never felt so alive as I have since coming to Wyoming."

Peggy's mouth stretched into a brittle line. "Amanda. We only want what's best for you and Marcus."

"What's best for me is to raise my son how I see fit." Amanda stood. "I love you both. But this is my life. My hope is you will come to respect my choice."

She picked up Marcus and strode back inside, leaving her parents speechless on the porch as the last rays of sunlight faded over the ranch.

Amanda let out a shaky breath as the screen door closed, leaving her alone in the growing darkness. She knew this wasn't the end.

Her parents wouldn't give up so easily. They had to understand she meant what she said. This was her home now. She would fight for it and for Marcus's future here, no matter what it took.

Marcus squirmed in Peggy's lap the following day, his usual exuberance subdued. He tugged at the scratchy sweater she'd put him in, fussing when she tried to smooth his hair.

"Such an active little boy." Peggy clucked. "He really needs more structure and discipline in his life."

Amanda bristled at the criticism but held her tongue. Ever since her parents' arrival, Marcus had been unsettled and clingy. He clearly wasn't comfortable around these strangers who were trying to impose their will.

When Brady arrived for his usual afternoon visit, Marcus broke into a huge smile and reached for him. Brady scooped him up, chuckling as Marcus babbled excitedly.

"Hey there, buddy! Did you miss me?"

Peggy pursed her lips in disapproval at Brady's casual familiarity. Marcus snuggled into Brady's shoulder, casting wary glances back at Peggy.

Later, Brady found himself alone on the porch with Reginald, who was scowling into his brandy.

"So, you're the ranch hand my daughter seems so fond of," Reginald said.

Brady bristled at his dismissive tone. "We're

friends. I help out around here when I can. She works too hard running this place solo."

"Yes, well, we'll be taking care of that soon enough," Reginald replied. "This is no life for a woman of her breeding. She belongs back east, not on some dirty, remote cattle ranch."

Brady felt his jaw tighten, anger rising, though he kept his voice even. "This ranch is Amanda's dream, Mr. Aldrich. She's worked hard to build a life here. You should be proud of her grit and determination."

The older man snorted. "Grit? Don't be absurd. She's sowing her wild oats before settling down properly." He took a sip of brandy, eyeing Brady. "I'd suggest you not get too attached to this little fantasy life she's created."

Brady clenched his fists, biting back a heated retort. How dare this pompous snob dismiss everything Amanda had accomplished? He wanted to tell Reginald exactly what he thought of him, but he held back for her sake.

"With all due respect, sir, I think you underestimate your daughter. She's strong and capable of deciding her own future. As a friend, I intend to support her, whatever she chooses."

Reginald's eyes narrowed coldly. "We'll see about that." Standing, he brushed past Brady, and stormed into the house.

Brady watched him go, shaken by the confrontation. A deep unease settled over him about what Amanda's parents might do next. But he meant what he told Reginald. He would stand by his friend.

Amanda stepped out onto the porch, her features a mask of misery. She'd overheard the tense exchange between her father and Brady. Though his loyalty touched her, she also felt a pang of embarrassment over her father's condescending attitude.

"I'm so sorry," she said, not meeting his eyes.

Brady gave her a reassuring smile. "Don't worry about it. I know they're just looking out for you in their own way."

She sighed, leaning against the porch rail. "It's more than that. They've never approved of me living out here. They think I'm wasting my potential."

She looked out at the distant mountains, her expression conflicted. "All my life, they've tried to mold me into their idea of a proper young woman. But this ranch is my dream, my purpose. I won't give it up."

Brady stepped closer, his voice gentle. "I know. And you shouldn't have to. This is your life. You should live it how you want."

Amanda turned to him, her eyes glistening with emotion. "Thank you. I'm glad you understand."

Brady reached out and squeezed her hand, a gesture of support and solidarity. For a moment, they stood together in silence.

The screen door banged open, startling them. Peggy Aldrich stepped out, eyeing their joined hands. Her lips pressed into a disapproving line. Amanda pulled her hand away, her cheeks reddening.

"Amanda, your father would like to speak with you," Peggy said coolly. She glanced at Brady, her gaze frosty. "Mr. Blackwolf, it's been a long day."

The dismissal in her tone was unmistakable. He tipped his hat. "Ma'am. Amanda."

As he walked away, he felt Peggy's glare on his back. His jaw tightened, but he kept walking. He wouldn't let Amanda's mother intimidate him. Amanda was his friend. And Brady Blackwolf had never abandoned a friend.

Chapter Seven

Amanda awoke with a start, the silence of the house ringing in her ears. For a brief moment, she wondered if the last week had been a dream—her parents arriving unannounced. *Her parents...*

She threw back the covers and padded into the hallway. The guest room door stood open, the bed made. The kitchen showed no signs of her mother's early morning ritual of preparing coffee. Amanda spotted a piece of paper on the counter and picked it up.

Amanda,

We've decided it's best to head home. It's clear you intend to continue on this reckless path, despite our advice, and we can't bear to stand by and watch you ruin your life out of stubbornness. We wish you'd come to your senses and leave this place, but you seem determined to dig your heels in deeper.

When you're ready to be reasonable, you

know where to find us. Give Marcus a kiss for us. When the time comes, we'll wire money for his schooling.

Love,
Mom and Dad

She read the note twice, then crumbled it in her fist. They hadn't even said goodbye. Part of her ached at their departure. Another part, the stronger part, felt relief flooding through her veins. They were gone, and she could get back to the business of running the ranch without their constant criticism.

She thought of the horses arriving later in the day. They were the first step in the new breeding program. Excitement rushed through her.

The sound of tires on gravel drew her attention. Amanda moved to the window in time to see the UPS truck come to a stop. A minute later, the driver jumped out with two packages. She hoped they held the additional tack ordered a week earlier.

Heading to the door, she opened it as a young man set the boxes down. "Thanks," she said to his retreating back as she picked up the boxes and returned to the kitchen. From the return address, they were indeed the tack she required for the new horses.

Amanda didn't open them right away, focusing instead on coffee and a bowl of cereal. She didn't have much time before Marcus woke up, and her focus would change once more.

She reminded herself the two Morgan studs and

six broodmares would be arriving soon, and there was still much to prepare. Anticipation had her stomach churning, even as she finished the last of her cereal.

With perfect timing, Marcus cried out as she set the bowl into the sink, filling it with water. A smile touched her lips at the sound of his voice.

"Mama! Mama! Mama!" It had become his standard refrain as he bounced in his crib, knowing it would bring Amanda to him.

"Here I come…"

He giggled at her approach. "Mama!"

Changed and dressed within a few minutes, she followed as he walked to the kitchen. He headed straight to his highchair and stopped, looking at her.

"Hold on, little man. Your cereal is almost ready."

Lifting him into the chair, she let him use the spoon, knowing it would be on the floor and he'd be eating with his hands in less than a minute. Picking it up, she rinsed the spoon. This time, she fed him. In Amanda's opinion, this was the most wonderful part of her day.

She headed out to the barn, holding Marcus in one arm and a checklist in the other hand. With his help, she inspected each mare's stall, ensuring fresh bedding was neatly laid and the automatic waterers worked. She continued on to an adjacent stable with six stalls. A stud would be placed at each end, keeping them separated by several yards.

Same as the mare stable, this one had a pen for each stall. The pens could be opened by center gates to create larger areas for the horses to wander. They'd be moved to pastures for further exercise. Satisfied, she moved on to the paddocks, checking the fencing and scanning the pasture for any hazards.

The sound of an approaching engine pulled her from her reverie. A large horse trailer rolled down the drive, towed by Virgil's truck. Behind him, Brady drove his own truck with a smaller trailer. Amanda's pulse quickened. This was it.

She walked out to meet them as they climbed out. Six beautiful Morgan broodmares stared out at her from Virgil's trailer, their coats gleaming. Two Morgan studs were in Brady's trailer. Hope and pride swelled within Amanda's chest.

"Let's get them settled in." Virgil moved to un-latch and open the large trailer gate.

One by one, they led the mares into one barn. They were beautiful, with intelligent eyes and good conformation. The two studs were magnificently muscled, with a commanding presence. Virgil and Brady led them into what they'd dubbed the stud barn while Amanda did a final check of the larger barn, confirming the gates were latched and the mares secure.

"The facilities are going to work well for breed-ing," Virgil said, as the three met outside the stud barn. "I know the Bonner family trusts you to manage the horses."

Brady walked to the pens outside each of the broodmare stalls, keeping a watchful eye on the interactions between the horses.

As the gray stud was released into a paddock, a chestnut mare trotted over to one of two fences separating them. She nickered softly before retreating to the other side of her pen.

"Hopefully, those two hit it off and give us a foal next spring," Amanda mused.

"With any luck, this time next year, there will be foals galloping all over this ranch," Brady said.

The thought made Amanda beam. She could already picture the foals frolicking in the pastures. It would be a new beginning. A future full of hope and promise.

Amanda sighed, her expression growing serious. "I wish my parents could see how much potential this place has, how hard I'm willing to work to make it succeed."

Brady put a comforting hand on her shoulder. "You're doing this for yourself and for Marcus now," he said gently. "Not for them."

Amanda took a deep breath of the early evening air as she surveyed the landscape of Kicking Horse Ranch.

The rugged beauty of the mountains and valleys surrounding her always settled her. The ranch represented freedom to her in a way the confines of the family estate back east never could.

She glanced at the paddock where the two new Morgan stallions were grazing. The studs, sleek and muscular, were magnificent, as well as critical to the breeding program.

The mares, in their wide pens, also investigated their new home, taking an occasional look toward where the males grazed.

Brady came up beside her, following her gaze. "The new horses look happy enough. We best keep an eye on the studs, though. They're always more feisty than the mares. These two seem calmer than many stallions I've seen who've been put to stud."

Amanda nodded. "As long as they sire some healthy foals, I can handle their high spirits."

"Not alone, though," Brady warned. "They get randy when the mares are in heat. You'll want someone familiar with mating when it's time to put the stud and mare together."

"It will all be fine."

Frowning, he wrapped a hand around her arm in a light grip. "This is serious, Amanda. Until you've been through the process several times, don't put a mare and stud together unless someone else is here. An experienced someone." Pulling his hand away, he stared into the distance.

She shot a look at him, studying his profile. It was unusual for Brady to be immovable on anything.

"You're right. I don't have enough experience. Someday, but not now."

Amanda loved these animals, loved the connection she felt to them and to the land. She had to remember the bond she felt toward the horses didn't equate to experience.

Brady gave her a searching look, as if reading her thoughts. "You're doing the right thing, staying here. Don't let anyone make you doubt that."

His steady faith in her meant more than Amanda could express. She managed a small smile. "Thank you."

The sound of an engine had them both turning. A truck was coming up the drive.

Brady shielded his eyes. "Looks like Virgil, Wyatt, and Anson are here. Anson wasn't at the ranch when the Morgans arrived. I'm sure he's anxious to see what he got for the money."

Amanda took a deep breath as the three climbed out of the truck, trying to steady her nerves. Having the three intimidating ranchers on her property made her realize how much she had to learn before becoming a real stockwoman.

"Good evening," she called out with a smile as they approached.

"Amanda," Virgil rumbled, dipping the brim of his hat, lifting his chin at Brady. Despite his sometimes aloof manner, he was a kind man. "Anson and Wyatt wanted to see how the horses are settling in."

"Great." She gestured for them to follow her and Brady back to where the studs were grazing.

"Handsome rascals," Anson said, placing his booted foot on the lowest rung of the fence.

Wyatt let out an appreciative whistle at the sight of the sleek horses milling about. "Fine looking stock. With bloodlines like these, we'll have an excellent breeding program in no time."

Amanda smiled with pride. "Here's hoping."

Her eyes met Brady's, something passing between them.

Virgil nodded. "We have a lot of faith in you, Amanda. Just holler if you need anything."

"We're here to help any way we can," Wyatt added. "Right, Brady?"

"You got it." Brady touched the brim of his hat, eyes never leaving Amanda's. "I'll be here for whatever she needs."

Amanda smiled at Brady, grateful for his steadfast support. There was something special between them, a bond she hadn't expected but now couldn't imagine being without.

Surprising them, the lead stallion let out a loud neigh and charged to the end of the paddock. Stopping, he reared back, turned, and ran back to where he'd started.

"Oh, my," Amanda said.

Virgil caught her attention. "This fella's getting used to his new home. It's normal."

Brady seemed to sense her cautious optimism. "This is just the beginning," he said. "With a solid foundation, the sky's the limit for Kicking Horse Ranch."

His quiet confidence in her meant everything.

"What do you say we look at the mares, then head up to the house for some coffee?" she offered. "We've got a lot to talk about."

The men voiced their hearty agreement and started up the path with Amanda in the lead.

Chapter Eight

Wyatt found Brady in the horse barn at Whistle Rock Ranch, grooming the three year olds following their afternoon exercise session.

"Brady, got a minute?"

Patting the mare's neck and setting the brush aside, Brady nodded. "Sure, what's up?"

Wyatt leaned a shoulder against a stall. "I wanted to let you know I've been talking with Pop and Virgil. We believe it would be a good idea to put a man at Kicking Horse Ranch to help Amanda. We want you to go be that man."

Brady's eyebrows shot up in surprise. "Me? You're sure?"

Wyatt nodded. "You're the best choice. Amanda already trusts you, and you have a good understanding of the ranch. You'd still live here."

"I appreciate the opportunity, Wyatt. I wasn't expecting it, but I'm happy to step up," Brady said.

"Amanda will be the boss, but we want you to handle most of the day-to-day operations."

They discussed the particulars of the new role, with Wyatt answering Brady's questions. Brady took it all in stride. Working with Amanda every day wasn't an inconvenience at all. Plus, he knew she could use some help with Marcus.

After finalizing the details, Wyatt clapped Brady on the back. "Glad to have you over there. I'll call Amanda so she won't be surprised when you show up. Go on over when you're ready."

Brady nodded, anticipation and apprehension swirling inside him. "Will do. I'll head over to Kicking Horse tomorrow."

Early the following morning, Brady pulled his truck to a stop outside Amanda's ranch house, rehearsing what he'd say. He knew Wyatt had called. Still, she would have questions about him being on-site every day.

Amanda stood on the front porch, bouncing a giggling baby Marcus in her arms. She watched Brady park and climb out of the truck warily.

"Good morning," he called with a small wave.

"Brady. You're here early."

"Did Wyatt call?"

"He did." She set Marcus down. The toddler tugged his hand from hers, surging toward Brady.

"Hold up, little man." Rushing forward, he caught

the boy before he plunged down the steps.

"Oh, my gosh. Thank you, Brady."

He swung Marcus into the air, getting the expected giggles. "He sure is quick."

"He's a handful, for sure." She let out a breath. "I shouldn't have set him down."

"Marcus is fine, Amanda. You do know he'll experience his share of accidents, right?"

Wrapping her arms around her waist, she nodded. "I've heard. As his mother, it still isn't easy watching him fall down."

"I've heard it gets easier with the second and third child."

She laughed. "First, I'd have to be in another relationship. Anyway, Wyatt did call. Why don't you come inside, and we can go through the new setup?"

"Works for me."

He followed her inside, accepting the cup of coffee she set before him. When she got settled, Brady explained his new assignment.

"I hope this works for you."

Sipping coffee, she cocked her head. "So you'll be working here full time?"

"That's right. Wyatt believes you'll need an extra hand. He asked me to fill the role."

She chewed her lip, glancing at Marcus, who sat in Brady's lap. After a thoughtful pause, she met his earnest gaze. "It does make sense. You'll need a place to stay."

"Wyatt said I could stay at Whistle Rock."

"Well, that doesn't make much sense. Check with him. If he approves, you can stay in the downstairs guest room."

"I'll check with Wyatt, but I doubt it will be a problem. I know how important the partnership is to you and Whistle Rock. I'll do everything possible to make this a success."

"Thanks, Brady. I know you will."

Amanda awoke with a start, her heart pounding. She strained to hear what had jarred her from sleep. There it was again. Another loud crash coming from the direction of the barn. Jumping out of bed, she pulled on shoes and rushed to the window. She spotted Brady heading down the steps toward the barn.

Springing down the hall, she rushed through the kitchen and out the back door. Hurrying, she caught up to him. As they neared the barn, raucous laughter drifted out into the night. Brady flung open the doors and flipped on the lights, revealing half a dozen teenagers drinking beer in the open walkway between the stalls.

"What in blazes is going on here?" Brady thundered.

The teens froze, eyes wide. One boy tipped over an entire case of beer bottles in his scramble to get up.

"All of you, out! Now!" Brady bellowed, his muscular frame filling the doorway.

The teenagers scrambled to their feet and fled the barn, one of them vomiting in the grass outside. Brady did a quick check of the horses to ensure they were uninjured. Furious, he strode outside and confronted the teens who were attempting to pile into a pickup.

"Don't you ever set foot on this property again, you hear me?" Brady yelled. "These horses are serious business to us. You mess with them, you mess with us."

The terrified teens peeled out down the driveway. Brady shook his head in disgust while walking back to Amanda. She met him on the porch, shoulders sagging in relief.

"Thank you, Brady. I don't know what I would've done if you weren't here."

"You would've figured it out, but you shouldn't have to. Those boys were way out of line coming here." He ran a hand through his hair. "Geez. I should've called the sheriff's office. Those boys may not be safe out on the road. Wish I would've thought of that earlier."

"You did what you thought was right. I'm sure they'll be fine. I just don't know why they thought a private barn was the place to have a party."

"I hope they don't come back." He motioned for them to get back inside. "Idiots," he mumbled, closing the door.

Several nights passed without a return visit. On the fourth night, Brady was awoken by the sound of raucous laughter coming from outside. Throwing off the covers, he slipped into pants and boots before grabbing a flashlight.

Stepping outside, the sound of music burst from the same barn as a few nights earlier. He knew the same teenagers had returned, even bolder than before.

His jaw clenched in anger. After confronting them last time, he'd hoped they would stay away for good. Clearly, a stern warning wasn't enough for these reckless kids.

Brady turned at the sound of a door opening. Amanda stopped beside him, phone in hand. "They're back, aren't they?"

"Seems so. You stay here while I check it out."

"But…"

"Please, Amanda. You need to stay close in case Marcus wakes up."

She knew Brady was right. "I'll call the sheriff's office if things get out of hand."

Nodding, he strode to the open barn doors. Brady flicked on the flashlight, the powerful beam landing directly in the eyes of the startled teens.

"I told you to stay off this property," he growled.

The teens looked at him, then burst into laughter. "We've got plenty of beer. You can have a bottle and join us." The one speaking was tall, with sandy blond hair and a rash of pimples on his chin.

"You have ten seconds to get out of here before I

call the sheriff."

The tall boy laughed. "You won't call the sheriff. There's one of you and six of us. Why don't you go back inside and leave us alone?" He took a long swallow from his bottle.

"You know, going inside isn't a bad idea." Brady walked out of the barn, then closed and secured the doors. Walking up the steps to where Amanda stood, he kept his gaze on the barn. "Make the call."

She called the sheriff's office. Deputy Aiden Winters answered, his voice crisp and professional. Amanda explained the situation and handed the phone to Brady.

"Hey, Aiden. I warned them off the other night, but I had a feeling they'd be back," he said. "I'd appreciate it if you could send a deputy out."

"I'll head out right away," Aiden said. "Trespassing, underage drinking, and harassing livestock are no small matters around here. I'll make sure those kids understand there are consequences for their actions."

Within half an hour, Aiden's SUV, followed by a second one, rolled up the drive to the ranch. He and Deputy Noelle Crawford got out.

"Thanks for coming. They're inside." He led them to the barn, hearing loud voices and music.

Aiden studied the area, his sharp eyes taking in details. He looked at Noelle, who nodded.

"All right. Open the doors," Aiden said.

It took a while to book the six rowdy teenagers and secure them in cells. The loudest of the group was the tall, blond kid with a big mouth. He demanded a phone call. Aiden advised them he would call their parents, who would decide whether to let their boys stay overnight.

Brady had followed the SUVs to the sheriff's station. He'd watched as the two deputies loaded the boys into the back seats. Of the six, it seemed obvious two of the six weren't drunk. It was too bad they'd gone along with the idea of getting drunk in the widow's barn.

The widow's barn. It was the name the tall, blond kid used for Amanda when he was explaining why they'd picked her ranch. The boys didn't believe she would do anything about them being in her barn.

Standing in the entry, Brady decided he'd done all he could for the night. If Aiden needed more from him, the deputy would call. Walking outside, he slowed when a pickup truck rumbled to a stop. A tall, heavyset man climbed out, his face flushed with anger. Brushing past Brady, he opened the front door to the jail.

"Where's my boy?" he shouted before the door closed. "I got a call you arrested him for hanging around some woman's place."

Chapter Nine

Brady followed the man inside, knowing the deputies would deal with him, but cautious all the same. He had a sense the irate parent was the tall, blond kid's father.

Aiden stepped forward. "I'm Deputy Winters."

"I'm Carl Jennings. Where's my son?"

"Let's talk in private, and I'll explain."

Carl jabbed a finger at Aiden. "We'll talk right here. You got no right to be harassing my boy! They ain't doing nothing wrong. Just being boys!"

Aiden held up a hand. "I understand you're upset, but your son and his friends were caught trespassing on private property twice. They were drunk and harassing the horses in the barn. Living in these parts, you must be aware of how serious these charges are. I'm simply following protocol here."

Carl's face turned purple with rage. "Protocol? You're ruining my boy's life over some horseplay! I ought to..."

He took a step toward Aiden, fists clenched. Brady

moved closer, ready to intervene, but Aiden didn't flinch.

"Mr. Jennings," Aiden said firmly. "I suggest you calm down. Unless you want to join your son in a cell tonight."

Carl glared, clamping his jaw shut. A moment later, he turned and stomped back to his truck. The engine roared to life. Making a U-turn, he sped away.

Aiden watched the truck disappear, then turned to Brady. "Well, that went about as well as could be expected. I think the message was received loud and clear." He checked the time before setting a hand on Brady's shoulder. "Why don't you head back? There's nothing more to do tonight. I'll get statements from you and Amanda tomorrow."

Brady nodded, relief washing over him. "I appreciate you coming out. Hopefully, this will be the end of our problem."

Aiden and Noelle's handling of the situation impressed Brady. As he drove back to the ranch, he thought about the boys and how the reaction of their parents would influence how their cases were handled.

When he arrived at the ranch, Amanda was waiting in the kitchen, cradling a cup of tea. "What happened?"

Pouring a cup of coffee, he recounted the details. She listened, her expression tense.

"I'm glad Aiden was there to put that angry father in his place," she said. "He actually said, 'Boys will be boys'?"

He nodded.

"Unbelievable." She shook her head in disgust.

"I know, but Aiden handled it well. He was calm and professional the whole time. I think Mr. Jennings realized he wasn't going to bully his son out of trouble."

She stood, setting her cup in the sink. "I hope this is the end of it. We can't have those reckless kids endangering the horses."

Brady leaned against the counter. "It'll be okay."

"I know. I'm glad you were here. I'm not sure I could have faced those boys alone."

"You could've dealt with them." He shrugged. "That's why I'm here. To help you however I can."

Her expression turned thoughtful. "You know, when Wyatt first suggested you come here to help, I'll admit I had my reservations. I didn't want to feel like I was being taken care of or pitied."

Brady nodded in understanding. He knew she prized her independence and didn't want to appear weak or vulnerable as a young widow.

"Having you here has shown me how much easier everything is with two sets of hands. And it's not just the extra help around the ranch. I feel..." She hesitated, as if searching for the right words.

"Safer?"

Her eyes met his. "Yes. Safer."

She took a deep breath before continuing. "I want you to know I really appreciate you being here, Brady. It means more than I can say."

Warmth bloomed in Brady's chest at her heartfelt words. Coming from someone as strong and capable as Amanda, it was high praise indeed.

"There's nowhere else I'd rather be," he said sincerely.

Amanda gifted him with a radiant smile. Brady knew without a doubt this was where he belonged. Helping her weather whatever storms came their way.

Brady wiped the sweat from his brow as he repaired the broken fence line. Amanda was across the pasture, checking on the mares.

"Everything okay over there?"

She turned, motioning for him to join her. "I think one of the mares is coming into heat."

He hurried over to where she stood, studying the mare. "I'll give Virgil a call." He pulled his phone from a pocket.

Dialing Virgil's number, he explained the situation. Ending the call, he looked back at the mare. "He's going to see if Wyatt is available to ride over with him."

"My guess is they'll both come over."

He nodded. "Me, too."

As they waited for Virgil and Wyatt to arrive, they selected a corral and collected halters for the mare and stud.

Soon, Virgil's truck pulled up with Wyatt in the passenger seat. They walked straight to the pasture where the mares grazed.

"The one on the far right," Virgil said.

"Yep." Wyatt narrowed his gaze on the remaining mares. "The others are close."

Brady joined them, holding up a halter. "What do you think?"

"She's ready," Wyatt said. "Let's get her in the corral."

Brady entered the pasture, the halter and lead rope in one hand, the mare's favorite treat in the other. He'd been doing this for years, and it never failed to draw the horse to him. It didn't fail him now.

He led the mare out of the pasture to the corral, where Amanda stood with the gate open. They watched the horse for several minutes, monitoring her receptiveness.

Once settled, Virgil nodded toward the stalls. "Brady, bring in the black stud."

The stud barn had been designed with each stall opening to a pen. At the far end of each pen, a gate opened into the corral used as a turnout and for mating.

Brady watched with bated breath as the impressive Morgan stud entered the corral where the mare waited. Despite the urgency of the situation, he couldn't help but admire the horse's muscular physique and spirited nature. This was a prime specimen, selected by Anson for his breeding potential.

Initially, the mare was wary, pinning her ears back as the stud approached. Those watching knew not to interfere unless necessary. This was the natural way of things.

After a few tense moments, her demeanor changed. She turned her hindquarters toward the stud, signaling her receptiveness. The stallion needed no further invitation. He mounted her swiftly as the mare stood steady.

Amanda observed the mating with Wyatt and Virgil from just outside the corral. A part of her remained clinically detached, focused on the goal of a successful conception. Deep down, she felt profoundly moved witnessing this intimate rite of nature.

"They seem to be a good match," Virgil remarked as the horses remained coupled.

Wyatt nodded. "We'll know for sure in about eleven months." He grinned.

After a few more moments, the ritual ended. Keeping a careful eye on the horses, Brady and Virgil separated the mare and stallion. Brady secured the stud in his pen while Virgil haltered the mare, leading her to a stall in the other barn. Afterward, the four stood together outside the stall.

Amanda let out a relieved breath. "That went as well as we could have hoped. Actually, better than I expected."

Virgil gave a nod of satisfaction. "Now, we'll just have to wait and see."

They gazed at the mare eating hay in her stall. The mating was over. In less than a year, a new foal could arrive, changing the future of Kicking Horse Ranch.

Brady moved beside Amanda. "She handled it real well," he said.

Amanda nodded. "I have a good feeling about this pairing. I think we'll get a strong, healthy foal."

"I hope so," Wyatt said. He paused, seeming to consider his words. "The other five mares will be ready soon. We should decide how to match them up with the studs."

The men talked about the pairings for a couple minutes. Amanda had nothing to add, though she listened, absorbing as much as possible.

A short time later, Amanda and Brady watched Virgil and Wyatt drive away, today's breeding complete.

"It's funny how even the small moments can feel so momentous," she mused aloud.

Brady nodded. "I know what you mean. Within the next week or two, we'll witness this a few more times."

"Yes, and each time will be special."

They walked back toward the ranch house, the sky slipping from blue to yellow and orange.

"With everything that's happened recently, it makes days like today feel extra meaningful," Amanda continued. "Like we're turning a corner, moving forward."

"Yeah," Brady agreed. He seemed to be contemplating something. "Amanda, I wanted to say I'm real glad I met you and Mark. Coming here, helping you, and being around Marcus…it's meant a lot to me."

"I feel the same way, Brady. Honestly, I don't know if I could've kept this ranch running without you."

As they climbed the porch steps, a cry sounded on her phone. "Marcus…" both said in unison, then laughed.

Chapter Ten

Amanda stood at the corral, brushing her horse's mane when the roar of an engine broke the morning stillness. She turned to see a sports car approaching, wincing when recognizing it as the one who'd stopped a few weeks earlier. The man driving had come across as arrogant, as well as rude.

The car pulled to a stop and a tall, athletic man in expensive black boots and a pressed white shirt stepped out. He removed his sunglasses and strode toward Amanda with a cocksure grin.

"Good morning." He held out his hand. "I'm Lance Pearson."

Reluctant to accept his hand, she removed her gloves and shook it. "Amanda Swanson."

"I just moved into a place up the road. Thought I'd stop by and introduce myself."

"Good to meet you. I'm a bit busy at the moment." She turned back to her horse.

Brady emerged from the barn, removing his gloves. He approached Lance with an extended hand.

"I'm Brady Blackwolf, Amanda's ranch hand."

Lance gave Brady's hand a cursory shake before glancing around the property.

"Quite an operation you have here. Do you run cattle?"

"We breed and train horses. Morgans, mainly," she answered.

"Huh. Well, I won't take up anymore of your time. See you around."

With a tip of his hat, Lance climbed back into his car, made a quick U-turn, and sped off along the drive.

Amanda shook her head as she watched him go. "What a character."

Brady chuckled. "Yeah. As my mother would say, he seems a little too big for his britches."

Amanda gave him a knowing look. "My thoughts exactly. I've dealt with his type before. There were a number of them in Vermont. My parents were always introducing me to them."

"Mark must've been a big change from the boys at home."

Chuckling, she patted her horse's neck. "You have no idea." She led him back to the corral, with Brady following close behind.

There was something about Lance that didn't sit right, but neither of them were too concerned. They had a lot more important matters to think about.

The week flew by as Brady and Amanda matched studs with mares ready to breed. Virgil had returned for two of them. Afterward, he'd left the mating up to his cousin and Amanda.

Lance returned to Kicking Horse Ranch the following week. He found Brady and Amanda repairing a fence not far from the stud barn.

Spotting a two-ton black truck coming up the dirt road, it took a moment for her to recognize the driver. She sighed, not keen for another encounter after their first meeting.

Lance brought the truck to a stop next to the fence and climbed out, sauntering over to Amanda with a sparkling smile. "Afternoon. Got a minute?"

She didn't look up from her work. "I'm a bit occupied at the moment, as you can see." Glancing at Brady, who indicated she should talk to the newcomer, she straightened, taking a few steps toward him.

Lance leaned against the fence post, grinning. "I just thought I'd take a chance and see if you'd like to grab dinner with me tonight."

She leveled her gaze at him, returning his smile. "I appreciate the offer, but I'll have to decline."

Lance raised an eyebrow. "Playing hard to get? I like that."

"My life is complicated, Lance. Right now, I simply have no time for personal wishes. It's been so long since spending a day at the spa, I can barely recall the experience. I apologize if this appears rude, but my main responsibilities are to my son and the ranch. If you'll excuse me, I must help Brady finish this fence so we can move on to the next job."

She turned her back on him dismissively. Lance lingered for a moment, considering a rebuttal, then thought better of it.

"All right. I take your point. Don't think I've given up, though."

He climbed back into his truck and drove off, leaving Amanda to shake her head in annoyance. Lance's persistence was grating, though somewhat intriguing. Why would a man such as Lance, have any interest in a widowed, single mother who worked from sunup to sundown on a ranch?

Brady waited until they were almost finished with lunch before pushing his plate aside and pinning her with a meaningful look. "You should take a day off and do whatever you want."

"Excuse me?"

"You mentioned not going to the spa. Why don't you make an appointment and go? I can take care of the work around here for a day." He lifted his bottle of water, taking a long swallow.

Shoving her chair back, she shook her head. "Because there's too much to be done around here."

"Like what?"

"Well..." She pursed her lips in thought.

Standing, he took his cup to the sink. "The stallions have covered the mares. All we can do now is wait. Take a day, or at least part of one, and do whatever you want."

"What about Marcus?"

"Leave the little man with me. How hard can it be?"

A few days later, Amanda sat in Brilliance Coffee & Bakery, enjoying a blonde vanilla latte while reading a book on her phone. She'd spent the morning at Magic Hands Salon & Spa and now felt more relaxed and content since Mark's death.

The bell above the door jingled. Amanda glanced up and tensed. Lance strolled inside, the absolute last person she wanted to see.

Averting her gaze, she stared at the phone, hoping he wouldn't see her. It wasn't to be. Lance spotted her, making a beeline for her table anyway.

"Fancy seeing you here," he said with a grin. "Mind if I join you?"

Before Amanda could protest, Lance pulled out the chair opposite her and sat down.

"Where's the little one?"

Amanda eyed him warily. "Not that it's any of your business, but he's with Brady."

He held up his hands in mock surrender. "Just trying to get to know my new neighbor. Making conversation."

Amanda sighed. As much as she disliked Lance, she decided to be civil and humor him.

"Fine. What would you like to discuss?"

"Well, for starters, what's good to do for fun around here? Any town activities or groups worth checking out?"

Amanda thought for a moment. "There's the Spring Fling Festival coming up. The planning committee is always looking for volunteers."

Lance perked up at this. "A festival, huh? That could be interesting. When's their next meeting?"

"Tomorrow evening at the community center," she replied.

"Mind if I tag along with you?" Lance asked. "Maybe I could lend a hand."

She hesitated, but relented. "I suppose that would be all right."

Lance grinned in triumph. "Great! Well, I'll let you enjoy the rest of your coffee. See you tomorrow evening, Amanda."

He sauntered out of the bakery, leaving her conflicted. She disliked the man, but couldn't deny he was persistent. With a resigned sigh, she sipped her coffee and looked back down at her phone.

Amanda and Brady arrived at the community center on Tuesday evening, Marcus in tow. She spotted

Lance leaning against a wall near the entrance.

They walked up to him, unable to ignore the persistent newcomer.

"Amanda, Brady. Good to see you."

Brady shook Lance's outstretched hand while she nodded.

"Good evening. I'm going to take Marcus to childcare. I'll meet you inside."

"Shall we head in, Brady?" Lance gestured toward the door.

They entered the meeting room, taking seats near the front, saving one between them for Amanda. The men made small talk until she appeared.

As the meeting commenced, Lance jumped right in, offering suggestions and asking questions. Amanda noticed Brady growing more tense, his jaw clenching every time Lance spoke.

After the meeting, Lance turned to Amanda. "That was great. What do you say I take you to dinner tomorrow night so we can talk about the children's area?"

Brady stiffened, forcing himself to calm down. "I can watch Marcus for you, Amanda. You should go."

Amanda hesitated, then agreed to meeting him for dinner.

Lance grinned. "Are you sure? I can pick you up."

"I'd rather drive. Where do you want to meet?"

"How about Chez Rémy at seven? I've heard it's pretty good."

"Let's make it six."

"I'll see you at six, Amanda."

Retrieving Marcus, they walked to her truck in silence. She secured her son in the car seat before glancing at Brady, noticing his brooding expression.

"Everything okay?" she asked gently.

He grunted, his thoughts churning. She sighed, knowing this situation was getting complicated.

Amanda drove back to the ranch, her mind spinning. She glanced over at Brady sitting silently in the passenger seat. His jaw was clenched as he stared straight ahead.

"Brady, talk to me. What's going on?" she asked.

He let out a long breath. "I don't trust that Lance guy. Something about him rubs me the wrong way."

"I know he was somewhat abrasive when we first met, but he seems all right."

He shook his head. "There's more to it than that."

She waited for him to continue.

He ran a hand through his hair in frustration. "It's just...you're my friend, Amanda. I don't want to see you get hurt."

She reached over and squeezed his arm. "I appreciate you looking out for me. You must remember, I'm a big girl. I can handle Lance."

Brady nodded, his eyes dark with turmoil. There was so much he wanted to say, but the words stuck in his throat.

They soon reached the ranch. Brady carried Marcus into the house, setting him in his crib. He walked back outside, needing fresh air to think. His thoughts drifted to Amanda's dinner with Lance the next evening. His stomach churned with anxiety and an emotion he didn't dare name.

Later, as he walked back inside, she approached him. "Thank you again for offering to watch Marcus tomorrow. You didn't have to do that."

He managed a weak smile. "No problem. I hope you have a nice time. I'm going to head to bed. See you in the morning."

That night, Brady sat on his bed, trying to concentrate on the sports program he'd selected. His mother's words from their phone call earlier in the day rang in his ears.

"It's time for you to come home, my son. I've found a good Northern Cheyenne girl for you here. She comes from a respected family and will make a fine wife."

He'd tried to put her off gently. "I'm not ready for marriage. Besides, my life is here now."

She'd clicked her tongue in disapproval. "You said the job in Wyoming was temporary. Your people need you here. Don't forget who you are and where you come from."

His mother's plea weighed on him now. He was torn between his loyalty to his heritage and his growing feelings for Amanda. Not to mention his promise to her late husband that he'd watch over her and Marcus.

With a sigh, Brady shut off the television, pulling up the covers. Sleep didn't come easy.

The next morning, he didn't stop in the kitchen on his way to the barn. He worked for an hour before Amanda joined him. They completed their chores in tense silence, both preoccupied with their own thoughts.

As he prepared one of the horses for an hour of exercise, Amanda came up beside him. "Thanks again for watching Marcus tonight."

He nodded, not meeting her eyes. "Sure. Anytime."

Amanda studied him with concern. "Is everything okay? You seem a little off today."

"Everything's fine," Brady said quickly. Too quickly.

She didn't look convinced, but didn't push it. An awkward silence fell between them once more.

After finishing up the chores, Brady held Marcus, both waving as Amanda drove off to meet Lance. When her taillights were out of sight, he sighed and went inside to fix dinner for Marcus. It was going to be a long night.

Chapter Eleven

Amanda arrived back home later that evening, exhausted and relieved. Brady glanced up from reading the latest issue of Western Horseman.

"Hey, you're back early." He set the magazine down and stood.

"Yeah, Lance had to cut the evening short. A work emergency of some sort." She slid onto the sofa with a sigh of relief.

"So, how was it?"

"It was fine. The food was good. Lance was...charming, I guess."

Brady tensed as he sat back down.

"He talked about working virtually, his impressions of Brilliance, asked about breeding Morgans. Anyway, enough about my boring date. How was Marcus? Any trouble getting him to sleep?"

"Nah, he was an angel, as always," Brady said. "He went down about seven."

"Bless you. I don't know what I'd do without you."

Brady chuckled. "You don't need Lance, or any

other man, Amanda. You're doing just fine on your own."

She looked at him in surprise. "What's that supposed to mean?"

Brady backpedaled. "Nothing, just that you're strong and independent. You don't need to depend on someone else."

"Even independent women need companionship."

So do independent men, he thought, standing. "Well, I'm heading to bed. Early morning tomorrow and all."

She watched him stalk toward the hall. "Thanks again for watching Marcus."

"Anytime." He hesitated. "See you in the morning."

"Goodnight, Brady."

Exhausted, it didn't take her more than a few minutes to head to her own bedroom. Closing the door behind her, she thought of Brady, perplexed by his odd behavior. She was too tired to put much thought into it tonight. It would have to be left for another time.

Amanda woke early the next morning, checked on Marcus, then made her way to the mares' barn. As she tossed hay into their feed bins, her thoughts drifted back to her conversation with Brady. She valued his friendship and didn't want to jeopardize it. If he'd just tell her what was wrong, she'd do whatever it took to make everything right.

He soon joined her in the barn, carrying a wide awake Marcus, who held his arms out to Amanda. Taking him, she snuggled his neck, making her son laugh.

Brady took over for her, working in strained silence for a while.

She walked to him. "About last night. I'm sorry if I said something to upset you."

He shook his head, not meeting her distressed gaze. "You didn't. It's my problem, not yours."

"Well, talk to me. We're friends, aren't we?"

Glancing at her, he nodded. "Yes, we are. It's just...you and Lance. I know it's none of my business, but..."

"You don't trust him."

"I think he's arrogant and self-serving. He's not interested in you. Not really." Brady released a heated breath, shaking his head. "I'm sorry, Amanda. I shouldn't have said that."

She set Marcus on the ground, clutching his hand. "You're probably right about him. The thing is, I need to figure it out for myself."

"I know. I just worry about you, that's all."

A grim smile lifted the corners of her mouth. "I know. And I appreciate it, I really do. You do know your job isn't to protect me, right?"

Brady chuckled. "I'll always want to protect you. It's the way things are."

They gazed at each other, the air charged between them. Just when he was going to get back to work, the sound of an approaching engine broke the spell.

Amanda picked up Marcus and stepped out of the barn enough to see Lance's truck coming toward her. She checked her phone to see it was before eight in the morning.

"Good morning!" Lance called as he climbed out. "Hope I'm not interrupting anything."

Brady's jaw tightened.

She plastered on a smile. "It's a little early for you, isn't it?" It seemed obvious he was interrupting their morning chores. At least it would seem so to most people, she thought.

Lance nodded, his eyes flickering between them. "Nah. I get up about five every morning. I just wanted to see if you'd like to grab lunch later."

Hyperaware of Brady standing close by, she shook her head. "Not today."

Lance beamed. "You pick a day, and I'll calendar it."

"I'll have to let you know. Now, we need to get back to work."

"Fair enough. Enjoy your day...both of you." With a wave, Lance headed back to his truck and drove off.

Amanda turned to look at Brady. "I'm pretty sure he's certifiable."

Brady grimaced, shook his head, and stalked off without another word.

She watched him go, an uneasy feeling in her stomach. She didn't like the obvious tension streaming between them since Lance showed up in Brilliance.

With a sigh, she headed into the house with Marcus, trying not to overthink things. She and Brady were friends, after all.

Brady used a special tool to repair a section of fence along the western pasture when he spotted the sheriff department's SUV on the drive to Amanda's house. He rested his forearms across the top rail and watched Deputy Winters and Sheriff Duggan pull up and step out, their expressions grim.

"Afternoon, Aiden, Garth," Brady greeted them. "What brings you by?"

Winters's jaw was tight. "There was a robbery at BK's last night. Two witnesses put you at the scene."

Brady's stomach dropped. "Robbery?" He set down the tool, then removed his gloves. "No way, I was here all night looking after Marcus for Amanda."

Duggan removed his hat, his eyes steady on Brady. "Need you to come down to the station. Got some questions that need answering."

"Are you arresting me, Garth?"

"No. We just have some questions."

"Then ask them here. You'll get the same answers here as at the jail."

"We have two witnesses who put you at BK's last

night around seven," the sheriff told him.

"What does BK say?' Brady asked.

Aiden spoke up. "He wasn't there when the robbery occurred."

"Who are these witnesses who said they saw me?"

Garth and Aiden exchanged unsettling glances. "We can't say, Brady," the sheriff answered.

"I'll let Amanda know, then follow you down."

"You'll come with us in the SUV," Aiden said. "You can call Amanda from the station."

At the station, Brady stood behind the one-way glass as Carl and Mickey Jennings stared at him in the lineup.

"That's him right there," Carl growled, jabbing his finger at Brady. "I'd know that face anywhere." Mickey nodded, glaring at Brady with undisguised malice.

"The fourth man from the right?" Aiden asked.

"I already told you that," Carl snarled. "That's the man who robbed the Gas & Get."

In the interrogation room, Brady sat across from Winters and Duggan as they grilled him about his alibi.

"Babysitting the Swanson boy doesn't prove your whereabouts," Winters said. "What we need is someone who saw you there at the time of the robbery."

Brady rubbed his temples. "I don't know what else to tell you. I didn't rob the store. I was alone with Marcus at Amanda's house when the robbery happened."

Duggan leaned forward, his eyes boring into Brady's. "This will get real serious fast unless you start cooperating."

Brady's unflinching gaze met the sheriff's. "I am cooperating. But I can't admit to something I didn't do."

The two lawmen exchanged a look. Winters slapped his notebook closed.

Brady took a deep breath, trying to keep his composure. He knew Carl and Mickey had it out for him ever since the incident with Mickey at the ranch, but he never imagined they'd try to pin a robbery on him.

"Look," Brady said, holding his hands open in front of him. "I'll tell you everything I know. I was at the Swanson ranch last night babysitting Amanda's son, Marcus. We watched a movie, and then I tucked him into bed a little after seven. Amanda called to check in a few minutes before seven. She talked to me, then Marcus, for a few minutes before hanging up. You can ask her to confirm."

Duggan scribbled some notes down, then looked back up at Brady. "And after the boy was in bed? Did anyone witness your whereabouts afterward?"

Brady shook his head. "No, sir. I read Western Horseman until Amanda got home about eight." He shifted in the seat, forcing down his growing rage. "I swear to you, I did not leave the house all night, much less drive into town and rob a store. What would I have done with Marcus?"

Winters studied Brady closely. They were friends. The deputy hoped they'd still be when this was over. "No offense, but your word doesn't mean much without someone to back it up."

Frustration welled up in Brady. He had no idea how he was going to prove where he'd been. But there was no way he was going down for something he didn't do.

"After what happened at the ranch with Mickey Jennings, you don't have even a small sense he and his father are lying to get back at me?"

Aiden had thought the same, but he didn't respond. Instead, he and Garth excused themselves and stepped into the hall.

Aiden flipped through his notes. "The store clerk just said the guy was big and wearing a hoodie. The witnesses said the same. A big Native American fella in a hoodie. But he didn't give a height or build or anything specific."

The sheriff looked at his own notes. "The clerk said it was black, and Carl Jennings said it was light gray. Mickey Jennings said it was blue."

Sheriff Duggan nodded. "Their stories don't line up exactly. And Brady is right about the Jennings having an axe to grind after we busted Mickey out at Kicking Horse. It's interesting the robbery occurred when BJ was off at supper. Any of the locals would know he wouldn't be there at seven. He never wavers from his routine."

The hall door opened, and Cindy, the dispatch operator, walked toward them. "BK Taylor is here." BK stood behind her.

"Hey there, Garth. Sorry to interrupt." He nodded at Brady. "Just wanted to let you know Brady here was definitely not at my store when it got robbed."

Duggan frowned. "And how can you be so sure of that?"

BK shrugged. "Because I was there the whole time it went down. I was in the back doing inventory when it happened. Didn't see who done it, but I know Brady wasn't there. My cameras caught the guy in the hoodie and the black pickup he drove. Brady's truck is white."

"You'll swear to this, BK?" Garth asked.

"I will, and you can see what the camera captured for yourself. I have to get going. You should let Brady go and find the real robber."

Amanda passed BK as he left the sheriff's station, a determined look on her face. Deputy Winters and Sheriff Duggan looked up in surprise as she strode up to them.

"I'm here about Brady Blackwolf," she stated without preamble. "You've made a mistake bringing him in. Brady would never rob a store or hurt anyone."

Duggan sighed. "We didn't have a choice, Amanda. Two witnesses said otherwise."

"Carl and Mickey Jennings? How convenient." She glared at the sheriff and Aiden.

"You're right in thinking they may not have been up front with us," Garth said. "BK just confirmed what Brady told us. If you'll wait out front, I'll bring him out."

Aiden felt a wave of déjà vu, recalling when he'd questioned the woman who was now his wife about a fire at Whistle Rock Ranch. Their relationship had worked out. He wasn't so sure the friendship with Amanda and Brady would have the same result.

The station doors opened again and a group of people streamed in, including Lydia from the coffee shop, Braydon Stiles, Virgil Redcloud, Wyatt Bonner, and several others. Anson and Margie Bonner walked in behind them.

"We're here for Brady Blackwolf," Lydia announced. "That boy has been nothing but kind and helpful since he moved here. There's no way he did this."

The other newcomers voiced their agreement. Winters and Duggan looked surprised by the show of support, and how fast the story had spread.

Duggan held up his hands to quiet the crowd. "I appreciate you all taking the time to come here. We've gotten some critical information from a solid source, and will be releasing Brady within a few minutes."

Amanda stepped forward, her eyes blazing. "Then you'll start looking for the real criminal, right?"

Garth's lips twitched. "Yes, ma'am. We certainly will."

Chapter Twelve

The crowd showed their approval with loud thank yous as they dispersed. Winters and Duggan exchanged a look before heading back down the hall to the interview room.

Amanda stood on the sidewalk with the Bonners and Virgil. "I don't know how this got so out of hand."

"The Jennings family are notorious for causing trouble." Wyatt held Daisy's hand as they waited for Brady to appear. "Mick has been in trouble since grade school. My hope is he moves away after graduation and grows up."

"It's obvious to me Carl is getting back at Brady for having Mick arrested. They're a pain in everyone's backside." Anson turned his steely gaze toward the glass doors as Margie restrained a laugh at her husband's description.

"Isn't there a law against false testimony?" Daisy asked.

"There is, and I hope Sheriff Duggan arrests Carl and Mick for lying about Brady robbing the Gas &

Get." Braydon Stiles kept his gaze on the entrance. "I'll bet he walks out any minute."

Braydon was right. Amanda and the others saw Brady emerge with Deputy Winters. His face was drawn, eyes shadowed. But they lit up at the sight before him.

"You've got a lot of friends," Aiden said. "Hope we can put this behind us."

Shifting toward him, Brady held out his hand. "No problem." After Aiden shook his hand, the two parted.

He moved swiftly down the steps to thank everyone. "I, uh…appreciate all of you showing up." Thanking everyone, he walked with Amanda to her truck.

She searched his face. "How are you holding up?"

He gave a weary smile. "I've been better. I'm just glad BK had cameras going when the robbery took place. Aiden said BK was in the back room when the robbery occurred. He didn't hear a thing until it was all over." Brady chuckled. "Guess he left out the back door and drove home for dinner before returning. Missed the whole thing, including Aiden and Garth showing up."

"We'll have to find a way to thank BK."

Brady's expression softened. He opened his mouth to reply when the station door banged open. Sheriff Duggan strode out, features hard as stone.

"Just got a call," he bit out. "There's been another robbery. At a quick stop on the highway to Jackson. Same dark hoodie and black truck. Two of my deputies are on it."

Brady positioned the heavy feed sack over his shoulder, hauling it to the barn. Amanda was already there, dumping flakes of hay into the feed bins of each stall.

"Morning," he said, setting down the sack with a thud. It had been two days, and the impact of the interrogation still clung to him.

She glanced up, a smile crinkling the corners of her eyes. "Hey, there. I wanted to get the horses fed before Marcus woke up."

"I hear you. I'll take care of the grain if you want to check on him." Grabbing a scoop, he distributed high-nutrition, low-carb, low-sugar grain on top of the flakes of hay. When finished, he poured the rest into a plastic container, securing the top. He noticed she hadn't left for the house.

"Do you ever think about where you'll be in five years?"

She glanced at him. "With the ranch and Marcus, I try not to think too far ahead. I take it day by day."

"Yeah. I tend to do the same." He ran a hand through his hair. "It's just...my mom keeps talking about me going back to Montana, getting married. The problem is, I can't picture leaving this place."

Amanda studied him for a moment. She hadn't realized he was struggling with the same conflict she was—between family obligations and personal dreams.

"Have you told your mother what's important to you? Do *you* know what *you* want?"

He met her gaze. "I want to be right here. It's where I belong."

Her throat tightened. She knew how he felt.

They worked in silence for a few minutes, each lost in thought before Brady spoke. "You know, I started reading some of the Northern Cheyenne history books Virgil gave me. It's opening my eyes to my ancestors and the battles they fought to survive. My parents had already shared some of it, but the books go into more detail."

"I'd love to read them when you're done. It's important to understand where we come from."

He nodded, his expression thoughtful. For a moment, she imagined what it would be like if he stayed at Kicking Horse Ranch, both of them watching Marcus grow up. Then she shook her head, clearing the odd thought.

"Well, back to it," he said, breaking the silence as he walked past her to the other barn.

She watched him go before heading into the house.

Amanda focused on grooming her horse, running the brush over its coat in long, soothing strokes.

Straightening, she watched Brady ride another horse into the corral. His graceful movements reflected his years of experience working with horses.

Seeing him put the horse through the exercise routine always brought a smile to her face. When it came to horses, Brady had a special touch. It was as if he could sense what the horse needed.

Marcus fussed from his playpen in the corner of the barn. Amanda finished with the horse and went over to check on her son.

"Hey, little man, what's all this fussing about?" She lifted him into her arms. He curled against her, his tiny hands grasping at her shirt.

Brady had paused to watch their interaction. Amanda's devotion to her son was clear in every movement and every word she spoke to him. Brady found himself thinking about his own mother, who'd raised him alone while his father traveled to take whatever work he could find. The strength of the bond between mother and child always amazed him.

Setting Marcus down and taking his hand, Amanda glanced over to see Brady deep in thought. She wondered if he was thinking about his family in Montana.

Maybe, in time, Brady would open up more about himself. She wanted to understand what shaped him into the man he'd become.

Over the next week, Amanda's parents called twice to check on their grandson. At least Marcus was the reason they'd given her. They made small talk before hinting at the real reason for the call—urging her to sell the ranch and move back to Vermont.

When the phone rang at eight the next morning, she saw her mother's face, knowing what was to come. Hesitating, she took the call.

"Hello, Mom. Is Dad with you?"

"He's on the golf course, dear. I wanted to pick up on the conversation we had the other day."

Groaning, she gripped the phone tighter. "And what was that?"

"Your insistence on staying in Wyoming. It's not practical, dear," her mother said. "Raising a baby all alone, way out there. Don't you think it's time to come home?"

She kept her frustration in check. "This is my home now, Mother. Mark and I chose this life together."

"Well, Mark isn't..."

Grief swelled in her chest. As much as she loved her parents, they'd never supported her choices. She needed them to trust her independence now more than ever.

Taking a deep breath, she tried to keep her voice even. "I know you're worried about me, but this is where I need to be. The ranch, this town. Both are part of my life now. Please try to understand."

She could hear her mother's sigh. "If you insist on staying, will you at least consider hiring more help?

You're still so young, you shouldn't have to take this all on alone."

"I'm not alone. I have wonderful friends here who help me. And Brady has been a huge support." A warmth rose in her cheeks.

"Brady?" Her mother's voice sharpened. "The young man who works for you?"

"His work here is due to the partnership between Kicking Horse Ranch and Whistle Rock Ranch. We work well together, and he's become a good friend."

"Hmm." Her tone made it clear she suspected there was more to the relationship. "Well, as long as you're being sensible."

Sensible? Amanda sighed, deciding to change the subject. She wasn't ready to analyze what might or might not be happening between her and Brady. They had an undeniable connection. Beyond that, she just didn't know.

After they hung up, she felt unsettled. She wished her parents trusted her judgment. At the same time, their concerns about the ranch's future weighed on her. The same as the future weighed on her.

She was still lost in thought when Brady walked in from working outside. He glanced at her, brow furrowing. "Everything okay?"

She gave him a tired shrug. "Just family stuff. Nothing I'm not used to."

He stopped himself from asking more. "Well, I'm here if you need to talk."

His sincerity meant more than he realized. With Brady, she never felt judged or doubted.

After a cup of coffee, they fell into their usual rhythm of working the ranch, the familiar tasks and Brady's steady companionship settling her nerves. Wherever they worked, Brady carried Marcus's playpen, which the fifteen month old climbed out of within minutes.

"We need another solution for the little man," he told Amanda.

"I just don't know what. Preschool won't take him until he's a little older, and potty trained."

"What about hiring someone? I know a lady in town who might help out."

"I'm not sure I can afford someone." She grimaced. "The truth is, I can't afford not to hire someone."

"Let me know if you want me to call her. She's a woman from my reservation in Montana. Her husband works at the leather goods store in town."

"Oh, I've seen him. About your age?"

"Yeah. He's my cousin...somehow." He chuckled.

"Seems like everyone from your reservation is a cousin of a cousin of a cousin. So, tell me about the woman your mother wants you to marry."

"I don't know who she's thinking about. She said it's someone I knew in school." He straightened. "Heck, I went to school with a lot of girls. Most are married with children. A couple went off to college. Some are already divorced. It's her way of getting me back to Montana."

"Are you thinking of going?"

"No, and I told her so." He got back to work. "Anyway, let me know if you want the woman's name."

She glanced at Marcus, who had almost climbed out of the pen for a third time. He stopped when he saw her watching him. "I suppose it wouldn't hurt to talk to her."

When Marcus toppled out of the playpen onto the grass, and jumped up, giggling, they laughed with him. "I'll get the number, Amanda."

Chapter Thirteen

As they rode to town the following morning to speak with the woman Brady mentioned, Amanda found herself opening up about the calls from her parents. He listened, asking an occasional question.

"I'm sorry they're pressuring you," Brady said when she finished. "Seems to me you're doing a fine job running this place on your own."

"I'm not exactly alone. You're here. Honestly, I wouldn't be able to get everything done without you."

He offered a crooked smile. "As long as you need me, I'm here for you."

His words brought a rush of heat to her face. She glanced away, not wanting him to see how his words affected her. This time, she allowed her thoughts to venture beyond them being friends, to wonder if there was a chance they could be more.

Amanda was still thinking about their conversation when Brady parked in front of the leather shop. She recognized the young man behind the counter, though she didn't know his name. Beside him was a woman who couldn't be more than twenty.

After quick introductions, Amanda and Lucia talked in a corner of the shop. It didn't take long to learn the young woman was the oldest of six. She'd often taken care of her five siblings when her parents worked. In truth, Lucia had much more experience with babies than Amanda.

While they talked, Marcus toddled around the store, reaching for items on tables and giggling. When he made his way to the women, he grabbed Lucia's colorful skirt, looking up at her. Bending down, she lifted him into her arms.

She spoke to him in Spanish, which confused Amanda, who'd thought she was from the Northern Cheyenne reservation. She set the confusion aside, watching her son and Lucia interact. The woman was a natural with children.

They agreed Lucia's husband would drop her off at the ranch at seven-thirty, five days a week. Either Amanda or Brady would drive her to the leather store when Marcus went down for his afternoon nap.

She already believed hiring Lucia was going to be an exceptional decision.

Over the next few days, Amanda noticed subtle shifts between her and Brady. Their hands would brush while working and linger for a moment. Or she'd catch him watching her, only to glance away when she met his eyes.

One afternoon as a storm rolled in, they scrambled to secure things around the ranch. She slipped on the wet grass and he caught her, his hands steadying her waist. They froze, faces inches apart. The crackle of electricity was undeniable. The moment passed, and they carried on as if nothing had happened.

The same night, Amanda lay awake replaying it all. She could no longer deny her feelings for Brady ran deeper than friendship. The question was, did he feel the same way? And if so, were either of them ready to admit their feelings?

She didn't have long to ponder those questions. The following morning, her sister, Tiffany, arrived from Vermont for a surprise visit. Though happy to see her, Amanda was also wary. Tiffany had never approved of her sister's "reckless" decision to move out west after marrying Mark.

The first evening, over dinner, Tiffany's disapproval surfaced. "I just can't believe you're trying to run this ranch all alone," she said, shaking her head. "It's too much for any woman, let alone a grieving, young mother."

Bristling, Amanda fought to stay calm. "I'm doing fine. This ranch was my dream, too, not just Mark's. And you forget, Brady is here full time, taking on half the work."

"But for how long?" Tiffany pressed. "Even with Brady's help, you look exhausted. No one would fault you for selling and moving back east, where you have family to help."

She fell silent, stung by the truth in her sister's words. Amanda was tired, bone tired some days. And there was no denying she'd leaned heavily on Brady these past months. Even so, the thought of selling out on the dream she and Mark shared cut deep.

"Please promise you'll think about selling. We only want what's best for you and Marcus."

Amanda tossed and turned that night, doubts plaguing her about the future of the ranch. She wanted to believe in herself, but perhaps Tiffany was right. Maybe she was being stubborn and reckless.

A weary tear slipped down her cheek as she drifted off to sleep.

The next morning, Amanda felt unsettled and on edge. She avoided Brady's searching looks, throwing herself into chores, unable to voice her inner turmoil.

She took a day off to spend with Tiffany, driving to Jackson for lunch, sightseeing, and shopping. Her sister didn't mention selling the ranch, lessening much of the tension between them. They had a wonderful time, the same as they had before Amanda left for Wyoming.

The following day, Tiffany volunteered to help with chores. Growing up, they'd always had horses. They'd taken hours of lessons, with Amanda competing in western dressage while her sister preferred show jumping.

Each had done well, with Tiffany moving on to the University of Kentucky as a member of their equine team. Unfortunately, a riding accident in her junior year ended her participation on the team. She transferred to the University of Vermont, obtaining a communications degree.

Brady entered the barn, watching the women groom horses for several minutes. "Why don't you two tack up a couple horses and go for a ride?"

"What do you think, Tiff? Feel like riding?"

"I'd love to go."

After lunch, the women left on a ride lasting two hours. It gave Amanda the chance to show her sister more of the property, including spectacular views of the western mountains. During dinner, Tiffany had gone on for several minutes about the ranch's beauty, laughing with Brady as he told stories of his riding adventures.

A few days later, when her sister's visit came to an end, she pulled Amanda into a long hug. "Don't stay out here just to prove something," she whispered. "Come home."

Amanda watched the rental car disappear down the driveway, overwhelmed and uncertain. She had no idea what to do next.

Amanda moved from one chore to another after Tiffany left, her sister's words echoing in her mind. She knew selling the ranch, packing up, and returning to Vermont was the sensible, easy choice. She'd have family and friends to help with Marcus, and she wouldn't have to work.

But when had she ever taken the easy path?

Brady found her behind the barn, absently watching a group of horses run in the attached pasture. He studied her face, seeing the shadows lurking in her eyes.

"Everything okay?"

She startled at his presence. "Yeah, fine."

Her brisk response told him the truth. Brady waited, knowing there was more.

She continued to watch the horses, avoiding his gaze until the words tumbled out. "Tiffany thinks I should sell. Says, even with your help, it's too much for me."

Brady tensed. "What do you think?"

Amanda shook her head helplessly. "I don't know. I'm just so tired, Brady." Her voice broke on his name.

He ached to pull her into his arms, provide comfort and encouragement. "You're one of the strongest people I know. Do I think you can make Kicking Horse a success? Yes, I do. Tired is okay. So is being exhausted. There's nothing wrong with feeling overwhelmed. I guarantee you Wyatt, Virgil, and even Daisy, have felt the same way you do now. Don't focus on what you can't do, but what you can. After working alongside you for over a month, what you can do is impressive." Taking a step closer, he settled a hand on her shoulder. "Whatever you decide, I'm with you."

She looked up, eyes shimmering with tears. Brady held her gaze, willing her to see the truth there. She gave him a tremulous smile, her eyes glistening.

"Thank you," she whispered.

Finishing evening chores, Brady saw Amanda sitting on the porch steps, watching Marcus toddle around while taking glances at the sunset. He walked up the steps and sat down beside her.

"It's beautiful here."

Brady followed her gaze. "Yeah, it is."

They sat in easy silence as the sun dipped below the horizon.

"You were right about successful people dealing with feeling exhausted and overwhelmed. I'd never thought of it quite the way you described. Not that I'm at their level, but the concept is the same."

Reaching out, he placed his hand over hers. "Yes, it is."

"If I sell now, I'd never know the potential of the ranch. I wouldn't be a part of its success."

He squeezed her hand. "True. Someone else would benefit from all the work you and Mark put into this place."

"And you." She smiled at him.

"To a small extent."

He picked up Marcus, settling him on his lap. After a while, she cleared her throat.

"I'm not selling." Resolve steeled her voice.

"I never doubted it for a second."

She grinned back, turning her hand over to clasp his. It was the first, tentative step in the direction she hoped they were heading.

Releasing a breath, she turned to Brady. "I know keeping the ranch won't be easy."

"You're making the right choice. This land is a part of you. It will be a part of Marcus."

They sat in silence, the only sounds the flutter of leaves and her son's constant chatter as he played with the snaps on Brady's shirt.

"I can't do it alone. I'm going to need help."

"Anything you need, I'm here."

Amanda bit her lip. "It's a lot to ask. You already know work never ends on a ranch. You have your regular job at Whistle Rock..."

"Whistle Rock will always be there for me. For now, my life is here." Brady met her gaze. "With you."

Her breath caught at the intensity in his eyes. The air between them seemed to crackle.

"Brady..."

He reached out and tucked a strand of hair behind her ear, his fingers lingering on her cheek. Amanda closed her eyes at his touch, leaning into his palm. When she opened them again, Brady's face was inches from hers.

"Amanda," he murmured. Their lips met in a soft, searching kiss before he pulled back. "No matter what happens next, I'm with you."

Chapter Fourteen

Amanda leaned forward in the saddle, keeping her heels down as the Quarter Horse rounded the arena at a brisk trot. Her brows were knit in concentration, focused on the cues she was giving the responsive gelding beneath her. A light touch of her legs asked the horse to pick up speed into a lope.

The rumble of an approaching engine broke Amanda's intense focus. She glanced up to see a black truck pulling up near the arena, Lance Pearson behind the wheel. Though she continued working the horse through intricate figure eights and serpentines, she felt a prickle of unease run down her spine. Arrogant and self-centered, he'd called a couple times trying to get her to agree to another date. *No, thank you,* she thought.

She asked the gelding for a controlled, balanced halt in the center of the ring. Loosening the reins, she leaned down to pat his sleek neck.

With a squeeze of her calves, she turned the horse and loped over to meet Lance, who'd left his truck to watch her from the fence. He watched her approach with an appraising look in his sharp blue eyes.

She reined the gelding to a stop a few feet from Lance and swung down from the saddle in one smooth motion.

"Hello, Lance." She stepped to the fence. "What brings you out today?"

His gaze drifted over her dirt-smudged jeans and sweat-dampened shirt. "Hey, Amanda. Driving past and thought I'd stop. Glad I did. That's one fine horse you have there. Is he yours?"

"No, he belongs to a client. I'm putting some finishing touches on his training before he heads home next week."

"Impressive work. You really know your stuff."

"Hope so." She chuckled. "I've been riding for years. Started training horses and riders while in high school. I need to get him back to the barn and cool him down."

"I'll meet you there." Lance jumped back into his truck, following the fence line to the barn. He entered the barn as she arrived with the gelding.

"This is Dakota." She patted the gelding's muscular neck. "He's a Quarter Horse, perfect for trail rides and cattle work. Smart and gentle. Great for beginner or experienced riders."

Lance studied the horse intently as Amanda untacked and groomed him.

"Do you have any horses for sale?"

"I do. Are you in the market for one?"

"Two, maybe three, so there'll be a couple for

friends to ride when they visit."

She straightened, set the brush in a carrier, and studied Lance. "Have you ever owned a horse before?"

"No, but how hard can it be?"

She wondered if the smile he flashed her was the result of a special dental treatment. "There is a lot of work to owning a horse. First, you have to feed them two to three times a day. Do you plan to be around or will you hire someone? There are a lot of high schoolers who might be interested."

"A high school kid would work. What else?"

"They need exercise. I ride Dakota five times a week, on the trail or in the arena. I took him on a trail ride with my sister when she visited. So, you'll want to build stalls and consider adding an arena, a round pen, and maybe a hot walker. None of those are cheap to install. You'll need access to trails unless you plan to trailer the horses. I can set you up with a farrier."

He leaned against the wall of a stall, crossing his arms. "A farrier?"

"They trim hooves and shoe horses. Don't skimp on the fee. A good farrier can save you a ton of problems. Do you have a place for the tack?"

"Is that the bridle and stuff?"

She stopped herself from rolling her eyes. "Bridle, headstall, reins, bits, saddle, blanket. Everything you need to ride the horse. Plus, a harness and lead line."

"All of that for one horse?"

"Yep."

"What'll that cost?"

"It depends. You can spend a few hundred to a few thousand for a saddle. Just the saddle, Lance. The blanket will cost anywhere from under fifty dollars to a few hundred. It's the same for all the tack. You don't need to pay top dollar, unless you want to. You'll also want to have a lunge line. Just one for all the horses. Another necessity is a collection of brushes, curry combs, hoof pick, and other stuff. This is an example." She pointed to the plastic carrier she used.

"What about the horses?"

"What do you mean?"

He shoved away from the stall, taking a few steps toward her. "How much should I expect to spend on the horse itself?"

"Oh." She shrugged. "They also range in price." She gave him examples of what he should expect to pay.

"That's not bad."

"How good of a rider are you?"

"I've ridden a few times, so better than a beginner."

If this went anywhere, she'd watch him in the arena. "Better than starting from scratch."

"Show me what you have for sale, Amanda. I'd rather do business with you than someone else."

"I'll show you, but I'm pretty sure you have a lot to do before moving a horse to your property."

"Let me see the horses, then I'll take you to lunch. We'll swing by my place, and you can see what I have for yourself."

"All right. Let's go." She walked out of the barn, knowing he'd follow.

In a nearby pasture, Brady worked a young mare on a lunge line, asking her to move away from him in ever-widening circles. Though the mare was skittish, tossing her head and snorting, his calm demeanor and steady guidance soon had her relaxed and focused.

He'd seen Lance drive up, then follow Amanda to one of the barns. Brady didn't like the man for a number of reasons. Number one was his interest in Amanda.

Looking up, he saw Lance follow her to the small barn where they kept horses for sale. He wondered what was going on. "One way to find out," he muttered, walking the mare back to her stall.

"Let me show you Chance." The small barn had six stalls. It was the first barn Mark built.

She led a buckskin gelding out of its stall. "This is Chance. He's just over fifteen hands and is a real solid mount. I'll tack him up and show you."

As Amanda demonstrated Chance's steady gait and unflappable temperament, Brady stepped out from the shadows of the barn, joining Lance. They observed, though Brady had the sense Lance was paying more attention to Amanda than the horse.

The men spoke little as she moved from Chance to another gelding, then to the final horse.

After she showed off Goldie, a leggy palomino mare, she and Lance leaned on the paddock fence discussing the horses' merits. Brady stood several feet away, listening without offering his opinions.

"I think the mare and Chance are perfect for me. I'd like to get several riding lessons from the expert herself to get comfortable on both horses."

Amanda smiled, holding out her hand. "I think we've got ourselves a deal."

They shook on it. Brady shifted as he watched, a muscle feathering along his jawline before he turned toward the house.

She glanced at her watch. "Marcus should be down for his nap, which means I need to drive the lady who takes care of him into town."

"Why don't I follow you into town? We can grab some lunch and finalize the paperwork for the horses?"

She shot a look at Brady, who stood next to Lucia on the porch. "I'll let Brady know." Jogging to the house, she stopped next to them. "Lance is buying two of the horses and a series of lessons. I'm going to drive Lucia to town, then meet Lance for lunch so we can discuss details."

"You can't work out the purchase and delivery here?"

"Well, I have to take Lucia to town anyway..."

He blew out a breath. "You're right. Selling two horses is a huge deal right now. The ranch could use the money."

As Amanda went inside to gather her things, Brady strode over to Lance. "When do you plan to move the horses to your place?"

Lance lifted an eyebrow. "Gosh, I hadn't thought about that. Not yet, anyway. I don't even have a place to put them."

"Not a problem. We can offer boarding while you're getting a barn installed. The prefabs are great and don't take much time. If you order within the next week, you'll have it up and outfitted within a month."

"Right. Good idea." Lance looked over his shoulder, relieved to see Amanda walking toward them. "I'm sure we can work out those details today during lunch."

"All right. Lucia and I are ready to leave. Where can I meet you?"

"I figured we could try that new bistro next to Florals & Floats. Have you been there?"

She shook her head. "Not yet. I'll meet you there in about twenty minutes." She glanced at Brady. "We shouldn't be gone too long. Are you sure it's all right to leave Marcus?"

Brady nodded, his eyes lingering on her face and the way the sunlight brought out the hints of auburn in her dark hair.

With a final wave, Amanda pulled out of the driveway, Lance following behind.

He watched them go, his brow furrowed. Brady had a bad feeling about Lance, though he couldn't quite put his finger on why. With a resigned sigh, he checked the baby monitor app on his phone before heading toward the barn, hoping Amanda would be back soon.

Brady moved through the barn, checking the automatic waterers and tossing flakes of hay into the feed bins and stalls. As he worked, his mind kept drifting back to Amanda's lunch with Lance. What did they have to talk about that took so long? Were they just finalizing the sale, or was Lance trying to get closer to her? The thought made his stomach lurch.

Brady's bitter reflections were interrupted by his ringtone. Pulling off his work gloves, he fished the phone out of his pocket and saw it was his mother calling.

"Hey, Mom. What's up?"

"Brady, I'm so glad I caught you." She rushed on. "Listen, your father's birthday is next weekend and it would mean the world if you could come home for a few days. I know the ranch keeps you busy, but do you think you could get away?"

He rubbed the back of his neck, conflicted. He loved his parents and wanted to see them, but the idea of leaving the ranch right now made him uneasy. Still, this was important...

"I'll have to check with Virgil. I'll do my best to make it work."

"Oh, wonderful. Your father will be so pleased."

Brady hung up feeling torn. His gut told him not to leave the ranch right now, not with Lance circling around Amanda. She was a grown woman, capable of handling herself. More than capable of deciding what she wanted. Maybe he was worrying over nothing.

He got back to work, weighing his responsibilities to the ranch against his duty to his family. After a while, he finished up the last of the stall cleaning. The physical labor had done little to settle the debate raging in his mind.

On the one hand, his parents were expecting him. He couldn't let them down. The thought of leaving Amanda alone with Lance, even for a few days, made his chest ache.

Brady knew he had no claim over her. She was her own woman and could make her own choices—about selling the ranch, going home to Vermont, or seeing Lance.

No matter how he tried to dismiss his instincts, they were screaming not to trust the man. Maybe it was the way he looked at Amanda, as if she were a prize horse at auction. Or how Lance seemed to always be hovering around her whenever he was at the ranch.

Brady sighed, wiping his hands on a rag as he made his way to the house. He could almost hear his grandmother's voice in his head, urging him to listen to his instincts.

Grabbing his phone, Brady texted his mother.

I can drive up on Friday afternoon. Need to return Sunday. Looking forward to seeing you and Dad. Love you both.

His finger hesitated over the send button, doubt creeping in. Was he doing the right thing? With a deep breath, Brady hit send. No going back now.

Chapter Fifteen

Amanda secured the cinch on Chance, the buckskin gelding Quarter Horse Lance had purchased, giving him an affectionate pat on the neck. "Good boy."

She led the horse out of the barn, with Lance walking several feet behind. Stopping, she turned toward him. "Ready for your first riding lesson?"

Grinning, his gaze traveled over her, then moved to the gelding. "With you as my teacher, I'm sure I'll be an expert in no time."

She gave a slight shake of her head. "Well, let's get started. Do you need help getting into the saddle?"

Lance looked amused. "I can do it."

Handing him the reins, she took a step back. "All right." She watched him shove his left boot into the stirrup before swinging his right leg over the horse. He landed with a thump while trying to gain control of Chance. When settled, he flashed Amanda a confident grin.

"See. No problem."

She wasn't impressed. "Do you mind if I give you

a few suggestions?"

"Give away."

"When mounting, it will be easier if you hold the reins lightly in your left hand and grip part of the mane instead of the saddlehorn to mount. Try not to pull on the reins." She continued, giving him several tips to make mounting, while controlling the horse, smoother.

"Not a problem, teach. Now what?"

Forcing a smile, she hid a grimace, knowing this was going to be a long two hours.

Amanda stood with her arms crossed, watching Lance drive away after his first lesson. The arrogance she'd first thought of as humorous, had faded to annoyance the more time she spent with the movie producer from California.

She'd learned a great deal about him over lunch to finalize the purchase details of the two horses. He'd been involved in producing several movies. The work had allowed him to amass a great deal of money, resulting in his purchase of the custom home and five acres in Brilliance.

He wasn't shy about his opinions, his goals, or what he wanted. While sharing his history in California, he'd made more than one comment about how Amanda would fit in with the beautiful people in the industry. He'd be glad to introduce her around and help her make connections.

Finishing her sandwich, she'd wiped her hands with a napkin and told him of her total disinterest in making movies or going to California. She'd been friendly, though firm. After today, she realized her indifference to his offers had gone over the man's head. Either that, or he didn't care about her opinion. Probably the latter.

Turning toward the house, she spotted Lucia coming out the kitchen door. She checked her watch. Without Brady at the ranch, she'd need to take Marcus with her on the drive to town. The sound of a vehicle approaching had her shifting toward the drive.

If she wasn't mistaken, Lucia's husband drove an older truck toward the house.

"I called him to pick me up."

She hadn't noticed Lucia standing beside her. "Thank you. I was just wondering about waking up Marcus."

"He's a good sleeper. I'll see you Monday." Lucia hurried to the truck, where her husband held the passenger door open for her.

"Enjoy your weekend." Amanda waved before heading into the house.

Her stomach growled on her way to Marcus's room, reminding her she hadn't eaten since breakfast. Tearing her gaze away from her sleeping son, she returned to the kitchen. Opening one cupboard after another, finding nothing appealing, she opened the refrigerator and grimaced.

Mouth twisting in indecision, she slapped together a sandwich, poured a glass of tea, and stared out the kitchen window. Taking a bite, she found herself wishing Brady hadn't left for Montana right after Lance had arrived. He always knew what to say after an encounter with the outspoken newcomer.

She wondered if Lance knew about her complicated feelings for Brady? Probably not. The man seemed to have little interest in anyone except himself. So unlike Brady, who rarely spoke about his family.

Finishing her sandwich, she walked outside, then came back in. Before the door closed behind her, she stepped back outside again. Resting her hands on the porch railing, she stared toward the series of barns. Three buildings holding the future of Kicking Horse Ranch.

Checking the time, she guessed Brady was almost halfway to his parents' home in Montana. Virgil had offered to send someone else over to help out. She'd declined, insisting she could handle the chores until Brady returned late on Sunday. The chores solved, she thought of the other issue on her mind.

She hadn't expected to miss him so much after a short three hours.

An image of his shy smile and kind eyes popped into her head. Amanda contemplated the flutter in her heart when he was near. It was the same response whenever Mark had been close. She wondered if this meant she was falling in love, as had happened with her late husband.

Abruptly, her parents' disapproving frowns crept into her mind, alongside her sister's skeptical raised eyebrow. They would balk at her affection for Brady, a ranch hand with no family fortune or a college degree. She sighed, sadness and frustration warring within her.

The ring of her cell phone jarred Amanda from her contemplation. Seeing Brady's name, she smiled and answered.

"Hey."

"Hey, Amanda, just checking in. How'd the lesson with Lance go?" Brady asked.

She rolled her eyes. "Ugh, that guy is insufferable. So arrogant and charmless. He spent the whole time bragging about his skills. Which are close to zero, by the way."

Brady chuckled. "Yeah, sounds like Lance. I don't know how you have the patience to deal with him."

"Me, either." She laughed. "I try to tune out the bragging and focus on the instruction. At least he's paying top dollar to make up for that atrocious attitude."

"You didn't discount your fee as you usually do?"

"Not a chance."

They shared a laugh, the easy camaraderie warming her heart. She was struck again by how in sync their perspectives were. Ending the call, she shook her head, knowing she was venturing into dangerous territory with her growing affection for Brady. The head and heart were at war, and she had no idea which would win out.

Ending the call, feeling much better after talking with Brady, she checked on Marcus, then headed toward the small barn. She ticked off what needed to be done.

Her phone rang again, interrupting her mental checklist. She saw it was Dr. Dorie Worrel and answered.

"Hi, Amanda, it's Dorie Worrel. I wanted to check in on those Morgan mares you bred last month. Do you have some time for me to come take a look at them today?"

"Of course, Dr. Worrel," she replied. "My afternoon is wide open."

"That would be perfect. See you then."

She smiled as the call ended. Brady had asked her to call Dorie before he left for Montana, both of them eager for the veterinarian's assessment of the mares' health. Their successful breeding had been a long-awaited milestone for the ranch.

Hearing Marcus's voice on her monitor, she headed inside. He bounced in his crib, with a huge smile, which turned to giggles when she appeared. Changing him, she grabbed a bottle filled with juice before stepping onto the porch.

Dr. Worrel's truck came into sight, trailed by a cloud of dust at three o'clock. Carrying Marcus, she walked out to meet her, exchanging pleasantries as they headed toward the stables.

The vet examined each Morgan mare, checking vitals and feeling for any abnormalities. Amanda hovered nearby, watching and asking questions, which Doc Worrel answered in detail, taking her time to make sure Amanda understood.

After inspecting all six mares, Dr. Worrel stepped back with a smile. "They all appear healthy. You've been taking excellent care of them." She slid her tablet into its case. "Any more questions?"

"None right now." She thanked Dorie again. As Dr. Worrel packed her bag, Amanda's gaze drifted back to the mares. With Brady's encouragement, she'd taken a leap of faith pursuing this breeding program. Success felt within reach.

Watching as Dorie drove away, her thoughts swirled with uncertainty once more. The ups and downs of the day mirrored the emotional rollercoaster she felt about Brady.

Pausing on the porch, she felt much better than she had before Brady's call and Dorie's visit. She took Marcus inside, the day's events no longer weighing on her mind.

Fixing Marcus his dinner, she fed him before unloading the dishwasher and starting a grocery list. The shrill ring of the phone made Amanda jump. She glanced at the caller ID. *Brady.* Sudden nerves gripped her stomach.

"Hey, Amanda. It's Brady."

"Hey. Glad you called."

"Just wanted to check in and see how the rest of your day went after our chat earlier."

Her pulse quickened. "Oh, it was fine. Doc Worrel came by to examine the mares and gave them a clean bill of health."

"That's great news." An awkward beat passed between them.

"How was the trip? You are at your parents' house, right?"

"Yep. All's good. How's Marcus?"

"Great, as always."

Brady waited for her to continue. When she didn't, he spoke up. "You're sure everything is all right?"

"Yes...it's just..."

"Amanda? You still there?"

"I'm here. Um...tell your father happy birthday for me. Maybe they can come down here sometime."

"Maybe. We'll talk when I get back to the ranch." A few seconds ticked by before she replied.

"Sounds like a storm blowing in. I'd better let you go, Brady. Thanks for calling."

"I'll call when I start back on Sunday. Enjoy your weekend."

"You, too."

"Hug Marcus for me. Bye, Amanda."

"Bye." She lowered the phone, wishing he were standing beside her instead of being a few hundred miles away.

Amanda put Marcus down for the night before making a cup of tea for herself. She stared out at the rain, lost in thought. Talking with Brady had stirred up a storm of emotions inside her. She could no longer deny her growing feelings for him, yet the potential consequences weighed heavy on her mind.

She already knew what her parents would say if she pursued a relationship with Brady. They'd always envisioned her marrying someone from their elite social circle back east. Brady was about as far from their world as could be. Her parents valued pedigree and status above all else. They would surely disapprove of a ranch hand with Native American roots.

Since Mark's death, she'd been focused on her son and establishing the ranch. Didn't she deserve to find love and companionship again?

Kind, hardworking, and honest, he was the same kind of man as Mark. Both understood ranch life and shared her dedication to the land. With Brady, she could envision a happy future for herself and Marcus.

She wished her parents could open their minds and see Brady for the man he was and ignore prejudiced assumptions. Even if they refused to accept him, shouldn't her happiness matter?

A soft cry from Marcus broke her reverie. As she hurried to comfort her son, Amanda came to a decision. She wouldn't let fear of how her parents would react hold her back.

If Brady felt the same way about her as she felt about him, no matter the challenges, a relationship with him was worth taking a chance on. It was time to listen to her heart and see where it led.

Chapter Sixteen

Brady slammed the truck door shut and gave a final wave to his parents as he pulled out of their driveway. As Montana faded into the distance behind him, he let out a long sigh. The drive back to Brilliance awaited.

At least he'd have plenty of time to think. His mind drifted back to his dad's birthday party yesterday.

His mother had spent days preparing the food for the event, and baking three of his father's favorite cakes. Brady had arrived in time to help set up tables, chairs, and decorations.

It shouldn't have surprised him to find his mother had invited Sandy Whittaker and her friend, Beth, practically forcing them at him all evening. Sandy was pleasant enough, and Beth was real pretty. The problem was, he just wasn't interested in either one.

He knew his mother meant well, so he'd let it go. The problem was being around other women his age didn't make him curious about them. It made him miss Amanda even more.

Brady shifted in his seat as he turned onto the interstate, the engine rumbling beneath him.

An image of Amanda settled in his head. Strong, passionate, a woman who could ride as well as any man at Whistle Rock Ranch. Always ready with a hilarious quip or a thoughtful word when he needed it. She'd been occupying his mind more and more.

A smile formed as the miles sped by, and with it the realization of what he had to do. His future waited for him in Brilliance, not in Montana or anywhere else. And he knew exactly who he wanted it to include.

Brady's thoughts grew serious as the first raindrops splattered his windshield. Dark clouds were gathering overhead, and soon, the rain came down in sheets. He flipped on his wipers, squinting against the sudden downpour.

A crack of thunder had him gripping the steering wheel tighter. This storm had come out of nowhere. The wind buffeted his truck as he struggled to keep it on the road. He slowed to a crawl, hunched over the wheel.

"Come on, just a few more miles," he muttered through gritted teeth. He was so close to home, but the conditions were deteriorating by the minute.

Lightning split the sky, illuminating the flooded highway before him. He thought of Amanda waiting for him back at the ranch, with Marcus asleep in his crib. The image helped him focus.

Mile by mile, he continued against the wind and rain. After what felt like an eternity, the "Welcome to Brilliance" sign emerged from the gloom. Relief flooded through him.

The rain showed no signs of letting up as Brady navigated the driveway leading to the house. Mud splattered his truck as he navigated the deep puddles pockmarking the road. Squinting through the downpour, he could just make out the warm glow of the lights in the ranch house up ahead.

Parking, he hurried through the deluge to the front porch. Shaking the water from his hat and boots, Brady stepped inside, welcomed by the smell of something savory cooking.

"Amanda?"

"In here," came her voice from the living room. Brady followed it and found her sitting up from what he assumed had been a nap.

Rubbing her eyes, she set her feet on the floor. "I'm glad you're back. I was getting worried with this storm blowing in. Are you all right?"

"I'm fine, just a rough drive," Brady assured her. "Didn't think I'd make it here for a while."

Her eyes shone as she looked at him. "You look tired. Are you hungry? There's stew simmering."

Brady met her gaze. "I could eat."

She busied herself tasting the stew, then gestured

for Brady to have a seat at the table.

"You must be starving after that drive." She ladled a generous portion into a bowl and set it in front of him, along with a hunk of warm bread.

"Thank you for keeping this for me."

She joined him with her own bowl. They ate in silence for several minutes, neither in a rush. Amanda wondered if now was the time to talk about her feelings toward him. Taking a closer look at his face, she decided to wait until another time. He looked up, catching her watching him.

They held each other's gaze for a long moment before she stifled a yawn.

"Sorry, I should get to bed. Marcus will be up at the crack of dawn as usual."

Brady stood, taking his bowl to the sink. "I should turn in, too. Long day tomorrow."

They walked to the hall together, pausing by the stairs. Brady leaned in and kissed her forehead.

"Goodnight, Amanda."

"Goodnight, Brady."

Amanda woke early, eager to get the morning chores started. Marcus was still fast asleep in his crib, his tiny chest rising and falling in a peaceful rhythm.

After getting dressed, Amanda heard Marcus babbling. Scooping him up, she changed him before heading downstairs. She could hear Brady moving around in the kitchen, along with the aroma of freshly brewed coffee.

"Morning."

"Morning." His eyes brightened at the sight of her with Marcus. The boy held out his arms, wanting Brady to hold him, which he did. He held the squirming boy for a couple minutes before Marcus wanted to be set down. "How about your chair, little man?"

Marcus reached for the high chair Amanda placed at the table. Once in the seat, she secured him before pouring herself some coffee. As she added cream and sugar, she noticed Brady watching her.

"What?" she asked.

"Just thinking how beautiful you look this morning," he said.

Her cheeks flushed. His open admiration was new and thrilling.

The crunch of tires on gravel drew their attention. They looked out the kitchen window, Amanda's brows furrowed in confusion as an expensive, deep red sports car came gliding up the drive. She wasn't expecting any visitors.

They exchanged a puzzled look before heading out to see who it could be. As they approached the car, the driver's door opened, and a tall, striking redhead stepped out.

"Good morning," the woman said in a smooth, confident voice. "I'm looking for Lance Pearson. I was told he lives around here somewhere."

Amanda glanced at Brady before answering.

"Lance's ranch is a few miles down the road. I can give you directions."

"That would be great, thanks." The woman flashed a grateful smile as Amanda explained how to find Lance. "I appreciate your help. I'm an old friend of Lance's. Thought I'd surprise him."

The vague explanation was all she provided before climbing back in her car. Without another glance toward them, she turned the car around and left.

"Well, that was odd." Amanda turned to Brady with a puzzled expression. "Any idea who she is?"

Brady shook his head. "Not a clue. She said she was a friend of Lance's. I've never seen her around here."

"Me, either," she said. "And the car she was driving was beautiful. She must be a real good friend to show up unannounced."

"Maybe an old girlfriend? Has he ever mentioned anyone to you?" he asked.

She folded her arms across her chest. "Never. I know very little about him. Did something seem off about her?"

Brady chuckled. "Everything."

"You're right." She laughed. "I hope she's not trouble for Lance."

They'd stepped back inside the house when her cell phone rang. Pulling it from her pocket, Amanda glanced at the caller ID.

"It's my sister, Tiffany," she said to Brady before answering. "Hey, Tiff, what's up?"

"Amanda, hi!" The cheerful voice she expected

held an edge.

"You all right, Tiff? You sound a little...off."

"Oh, you know. How are you? I hope I'm not catching you at a bad time."

"No, you're fine. Brady and I are getting ready to start chores. What's going on?"

"Well..." Tiffany hesitated. "I know this is last minute, and unexpected."

"What is unexpected?"

"Well, I was hoping I could come stay with you in Brilliance for a little while. Maybe a few weeks or something. I need to get away from here and clear my head."

Amanda's eyebrows shot up in surprise. "Is everything okay? You were just here."

"I know, I know. I've just, well... I could use more time out there with you and Marcus. You know?"

Tiffany's request had caught her off guard. "I'm happy to have you anytime. Can I ask, why now? Did something happen?"

Tiffany sighed. "Nothing specific. After spending time on your ranch, the city feels claustrophobic. I know you're rebuilding the ranch, and I want to help. You know I'm good with horses, and I could help watch Marcus. What do you think?"

An extra pair of hands with Marcus would be helpful. Still, Amanda couldn't shake the feeling her sister wasn't being forthcoming about her reasons for another visit so soon.

"All right. When do you plan to fly out?"

"Three to four days. I'll let you know," Tiffany

said. "I appreciate you letting me stay a while."

"It's not a problem. I'm glad to have you. Travel safe and let me know your plans."

After a few more minutes of chatting, Amanda ended the call and turned to Brady with a conflicted look.

"Well, looks like I've got a houseguest coming. Tiffany wants to come out and stay indefinitely to 'Clear her head' she says. I've got a feeling there's more to it, though."

"If you want me to start bunking at Whistle Rock, I can move back. I'll still be here early and stay late. Whatever you need."

She wanted to spill out her heart and tell him her feelings about him. "I'd rather you stay here. I can turn Mark's office into a bedroom. It already has a sofa bed in it. Of course, it's your decision."

Brady nodded. "I hear you. Tiffany should be your first concern. Family is important. We'll make it work, don't worry."

She gave him a small, grateful smile. "Thank you for understanding. I just hope this doesn't end up complicating...things."

"What things are you talking about?" Brady watched Marcus roam the kitchen, babbling to himself.

Leaning against the counter, she struggled with how to answer.

"Amanda?"

He walked to her, giving her shoulder a reassuring squeeze. "It's gonna be fine. We'll take it as it comes."

Chapter Seventeen

"You know, why don't we ride to the northern pasture this evening," Brady said. "We haven't checked on the herd in a few days. It'd be nice to get away for a bit before your sister arrives. If you want to, that is."

Amanda's eyes softened. "I'd need someone to watch Marcus."

"I've a real simple solution." He grinned. "Sam said she'd be happy to watch Marcus anytime. She loves kids, and so does Logan. I'll call and see if they're available tonight."

"That would be great." She rose on the balls of her feet, kissing his cheek, feeling her face heat. "Um...I'm going to get Marcus ready to go outside. Be right back."

He grinned at the unexpected show of affection. "I'll let you know what she says."

Amanda released a slow breath as she carried Marcus to his bedroom. She felt a flicker of anticipation at the prospect of spending time alone with Brady. The northern pasture was one of her favorite places on the ranch. Riding there with him, away from reminders of everything still to be done at the ranch, seemed very appealing.

Finishing getting Marcus ready, she carried the squirming boy outside and to the closest barn. Brady had already taken care of the morning feeding. He'd led the horses into their outdoor pens, and had begun mucking their stalls.

Amanda was about to set Marcus inside the empty stall when she spotted Lucia's truck. The instant Marcus saw his nanny climb out, he struggled for his mother to set him down. He tried to run toward Lucia, falling once, then popping back up before being lifted into the woman's arms.

"Your timing is perfect, as always," Amanda said. "He's fed and ready to go."

"Thank you." Lucia held up a cloth bag. "I brought toys for today, and a new story." Without another word, she carried Marcus into the house.

Amanda busied herself with completing the morning chores, trying not to speculate about the upcoming ride with Brady. She knew he wanted to help take her mind off things before her sister arrived. She stifled a grin, deciding the ride would give her a chance to tell him how she felt. Her stomach already churned with butterflies.

An hour later, Lance arrived for his next lesson. Amanda had forgotten about the appointment until she spotted his truck.

"Well, rats," she muttered, at the same time lifting her hand in a wave. "Good morning, Lance."

"Hey, there. Which horse is scheduled for today?"

"Goldie. Do you want to watch me tack her up or do it yourself?"

"You go ahead."

"Follow me." She tacked up the mare, leading her into the corral, and handed Lance the reins. "Do you remember what I said about mounting?"

"Of course."

She watched him climb into the saddle, repeating all the mistakes he'd made the first time. Letting out a breath, she smiled before going over the basics one more time.

Sam and Logan arrived right on time, eager to spend the evening with Marcus. "Hope you have enough energy for the little man," Brady said, clasping Logan on the shoulder.

"I'll give it my best," he replied. "Sam's the one with endless energy. I just try to keep up."

After going over nighttime details with them, Amanda left to meet Brady in the barn. She tacked up her mare before leading it outside to find Brady already waiting, a bay gelding saddled and packed for the ride. They cswung up into their saddles and headed out.

Neither spoke much as they navigated the trail to the northern pasture. The silence between them was comfortable, both content to enjoy the beauty of the landscape.

As they crested a rise overlooking the pasture, she drew in a deep breath, taking in the sweeping vista of wildflowers and snowcapped peaks in the distance. This was her favorite view on the ranch.

"It's beautiful up here." Brady echoed her thoughts, gazing out at the scenery. "I'm glad we did this."

Nodding, she became very aware of how alone they were up here. It was just the two of them and the horses, isolated amidst the grandeur of the mountains. She snuck a glance at Brady's rugged profile and felt a familiar fluttering in her chest, a mix of nerves and excitement.

They guided their horses toward the small herd of Angus cattle, the animals grazing as they rode. As she soaked up the tranquil setting surrounding them, she could also sense an undercurrent of tension simmering between her and Brady. There were things left unsaid, a gulf of uncertainty neither had yet crossed.

"I'll drive up more hay tomorrow to supplement what's left in the pasture," Brady said. "We'll move them farther north in a few days."

"All right." She felt a jolt of emotion, telling herself the time had come to admit how she felt.

Brady reined his horse closer to her. "We should probably start heading back soon." He made no move to turn around.

Amanda nodded, desperate to get the words out. "Brady…"

His dark eyes were unreadable. "Yeah?"

"I wanted to say thank you...um...for suggesting this ride. It was really nice to get away for a bit."

He studied her face. She thought he might be about to say something more. Then he nodded.

"Of course. What are friends for?" He flashed a faint grin, then wheeled his horse around to start for home.

Amanda followed, chastising herself for not having the courage to go through with her plan. She hoped to be brave, put her fear of rejection aside, and admit her feelings. Instead, she let the moment pass.

She rode a few paces away from him as they entered the ranch yard, trying to settle the jumble of thoughts and emotions swirling through her. Their ride together had been peaceful, yet she'd failed at the one conversation she'd wanted to address.

Brady swung down from his horse once they reached the barn. "I'll take care of untacking these two if you want to head into the house."

On a reluctant nod, she handed over the reins. "Thanks. I'll see you inside."

As she walked up to the porch, her mind drifted back to the charged moment on the ridge when she'd almost blurted out her feelings. What would Brady have said if she'd found the courage to continue? Did he feel the same pull toward her?

Amanda stepped through the kitchen door of the ranch house, stopping when hearing laughter. The sound of a rodeo blared from the TV in the living room. Sam and Logan sat hunched over the coffee table, engrossed in an intense game of cards. An empty pizza box and two half-filled glasses of tea on the table between them.

"Hey, guys," she greeted, breaking their concentration.

"Hey, Amanda," Sam replied without looking up from her cards. "Marcus is asleep in his crib."

"Great." She laid her hat on a chair before checking on her son. Every time she looked at him, a spark of wonder shocked her heart. Such a beautiful child, and he was hers. After touching his cheek, she returned to the living room.

"Thanks again for watching him. Let me pay you for your trouble." She started to pull some cash from her pocket, but Logan waved it away.

"Don't worry about it," he said. "That's what friends are for."

Amanda nodded, touched by their kindness. Ever since her husband died, the people from Whistle Rock Ranch, and the neighboring Kelman Ranch, had become like family.

The front door swung open, and Brady strode in. Her pulse quickened at the sight of his lean, rugged frame. His dark eyes met hers, and her regret came flooding back.

"We should all get dinner sometime, my treat," Brady suggested. "It'll give us a chance to catch up."

He actually meant it as a way to pay them back for the time watching Marcus.

"Sure, sounds good." Sam stood, grabbing her light jacket.

"Let us know what works for you guys," Logan said. "Our evenings are almost always open. See you soon." He shook Brady's hand and kissed Amanda's cheek before following Sam to their truck.

Watching them go, Brady and Amanda fell into an awkward silence. There was so much left unsaid, so many buried feelings, yet neither spoke up.

"I'll be moving the herd to the northern pasture tomorrow," Brady said, picking up a bottle of water from the refrigerator. "I'll need to get an early start."

"I can help once Lucia arrives."

"Nah. This is an easy, one-man job. It won't take long to load the truck and drive it to the pasture. If I start at seven, I'll be back by ten."

Amanda nodded, avoiding his piercing gaze. "All right." They headed toward the hall.

Stopping at the base of the stairs for a long moment, the air grew thick with tension. Her heart pounded as Brady reached for her hand, pulling her close. She sighed as his lips met hers in a fiery kiss. His strong arms wrapped around her, erasing anything she might be thinking. She melted into his embrace, overcome with desire.

Long seconds passed before they broke apart, breathless. Her mind reeled. She saw the passion burning in his eyes, indicating the depth of his feelings.

Without a word, they retreated to their separate bedrooms, their newfound bond hanging in the balance. Changing into sleeping pants and a top, she slipped under the covers. Her thoughts raced as she lay awake long into the night.

Amanda descended the stairs the following morning, ready to get her day started. Making coffee, she poured herself a cup and looked out the kitchen window. Brady was almost finished loading the truck with hay for the herd in the northern pasture. Spotting her watching him, he waved, closed the truck's gate, and jogged to the house.

Brady strode into the kitchen, his commanding presence filling the room. His penetrating gaze found hers, hinting at the passionate kiss they'd shared.

Not knowing what to say, she filled a thermos with coffee. "Here. And be sure to take water."

Chuckling, he took it from her. "Yes, ma'am. Anything else?"

"Can't think of anything."

"Then you aren't thinking hard enough." Bending, he kissed her. Resting his hands on her shoulders, he kept her close for a long time before lifting his head. "That's better. I should get going if I'm going to get back here before lunch." He gave a salute before heading outside.

Not moving, she touched her lips, still feeling them tingle.

Amanda tried to focus on her chores throughout the morning, but her thoughts kept drifting back to Brady. The feel of his lips on hers, his hands resting on her shoulders...she simply couldn't shove them from her thoughts.

As noon approached, Amanda paced the porch, watching for any sign of Brady's return. At twelve-thirty, she spotted his truck coming down the road from the north. Her heart raced at the sight.

Parking, he climbed out, removing his hat to stretch and wipe the sweat from his brow. She set aside the halter in her hand to meet him.

"How'd it go?"

"Leaving the hay went smooth enough. I got a flat tire driving back. It took longer than expected to fix it. My spare is sketchy. I need to get a new tire. I'll head to Pete's this afternoon and have him change the spare out."

"Nash's Auto Repair is generally booked up. You may want to call."

He flashed a rueful grin. "Pete will fit me in. He owes me."

Her brows furrowed. "For what?"

"A small electrical fire started while I waited for

him to finish up my truck a few months ago. I put it out before it could do much damage."

"Do you mind driving Lucia to town when you go?"

"Not at all. Is she ready now?"

She shook her head. "She's putting Marcus down for his nap. I have lunch ready for all of us. Are you hungry?"

"Always."

He fell silent, scuffing his boots against the porch boards as they walked inside. The air between them grew thick with tension.

Brady studied her for a long moment, emotions warring on his face. Then in two swift strides, he was in front of her, pulling her into his arms. His mouth found hers in a searing kiss that stole her breath away.

When they broke apart, he rested his forehead against hers. "I've wanted to do that all day."

Smiling, she lifted a hand to caress his cheek. "So have I."

They stood wrapped in each other's arms until the sound of Lucia's humming floated into the kitchen. Putting space between them, he looked away when Lucia entered the kitchen.

"Everything all right?" she asked.

"Everything's better than all right," he answered, smiling at Amanda.

Chapter Eighteen

The afternoon passed slower than usual, with Amanda keeping busy by exercising the horses, and checking on the Morgan mares. It shouldn't have surprised her how often thoughts of Brady interfered with her chores.

Marcus slept late, giving her ample time to complete everything. As she prepared to head inside, the sound of an approaching vehicle had her turning toward the long drive. Hoping to see Brady's truck, her shoulders sagged at the sight of the familiar red sports car. The stunning redhead sat behind the wheel.

"Now what?" she muttered. Amanda considered ignoring the woman and returning to the house. Sadly, being rude wasn't in her, so she stood erect as the woman parked and got out.

"Hello!" She waved at Amanda, walking toward her. Her clothes today included skintight jeans, a tight lime green blouse, lime green and black boots, and several strands of colored beads hanging around her neck. On anyone else, the combination would look cheap. This woman was able to carry it off.

"Good afternoon. Did you find Lance?"

"Found his house. He's out of town. At least that's what the housekeeper told me." The woman looked around with a critical eye, as if determining if the ranch met her expectations.

"Are you leaving town then?"

"Ha! Not a chance. I'm staying there, until he returns, and we have a chance to talk."

Amanda eyed her, then stuck out her hand. "I'm Amanda Swanson."

Gripping it, the woman met her gaze. "Kelsey Kinneman. Nice to meet you."

"What brings you to the ranch?"

"Lance's housekeeper told me he bought two horses from you and you're giving him lessons."

"True." Amanda wondered where this was going.

"I'm certain one of the horses is for me. So, I'd like you to provide lessons for me, too."

She hoped her face didn't display her dismay at the assumptions Kelsey had made. "Well, I'm happy to give you lessons on one of my other horses, but not one of the two Lance purchased. Not without his express permission." She quoted the fee.

"The cost is fine. Lance will pay it. Can I at least see the two horses he bought?"

Not seeing a problem, Amanda motioned for the woman to follow to their stalls. "This is Chance. He's a Quarter Horse buckskin gelding."

"Oh, he must be Lance's horse. Right?"

"He's taking lessons on both. I don't know if he's made a decision." She walked to the next stall. "And this is Goldie, a palomino mare. She's half Arabian and half Quarter Horse."

"She's gorgeous. This one must be mine."

Amanda sighed. "As I said, I don't know what Lance plans. If you want a lesson, I'll be happy to teach you on one of the other horses."

Kelsey spread her arms out, making a swift turn. "Will this do?"

"Your clothes will work fine. My policy is to accept payment at the start of each lesson." She quoted the price one more time.

"That's nothing, honey. You need to raise your rates."

The comment caused Amanda's cheeks to flush. "I appreciate your input, but I've found my rate works fine for me and my clients."

Making a quick turn, Kelsey walked back to her car and took a few bills from her purse. Holding them in the air, she returned, handing them to Amanda.

"This is too much."

"No, it's what you should be charging, plus a tip. I know for a fact, that amount is what's charged around Jackson Hole. Do I get to pick the horse?"

Folding the bills, she tucked them into her jeans before taking a lesson agreement from a shelf. "Read and sign this, then we can get started. How much experience do you have?"

Not bothering to read the form, she signed and handed it back. "I've been riding since I turned seven.

Unfortunately, I haven't ridden much for the last few years."

"All right. I'll tack up Sugar for you. She's another Quarter Horse mare." Amanda walked toward the last stall. "She's a bit flashy."

"Flashy is my specialty," Kelsey said, gasping at the horse staring at her. "Is that Sugar?"

"It is."

"She's perfect. I accept your choice."

Amanda stopped herself from bursting out in laughter. Grabbing the halter and lead line, she gathered the mare, leading her outside to an open pasture.

Reviewing the basics as she did with every student, she asked if Kelsey had any questions.

"No. I'm ready to ride."

Oh boy, Amanda thought, handing Kelsey the reins. "Do you need help mounting?"

"Nope. I have this." Holding the reins, she slid her booted left foot into a stirrup, gripped a chunk of Sugar's mane, and swung into the saddle with the grace of an experienced rider.

"Very nice, Kelsey. Are you comfortable riding her in a circle?"

Without responding, she clucked and squeezed her calves enough to get Sugar moving. Amanda watched, impressed with Kelsey's skills. After an hour, she found herself wondering why the woman paid for a lesson she didn't need.

Brady returned close to five o'clock, several hours later than intended. Entering the kitchen, he inhaled the wonderful aroma of something simmering on the stove. Checking the oven, a slow smile spread across his face.

"Enchilada casserole," he muttered. Opening the refrigerator, he spotted a bowl of homemade guacamole. On the counter was a bag of fresh corn chips from a local Mexican restaurant. His stomach rumbled at tonight's feast.

"Thought I heard you. Was Pete able to fit you in?" Amanda glanced behind her, making sure Marcus followed, before checking the casserole.

Brady lifted the boy into his arms. Nuzzling his neck, he got the suspected giggle. "Yes. He also showed me the wear on the other three. Pete estimated I'd need to change them within a few months. He sold them to me at cost and labor. So it took a little longer."

"You were right. He gave you a real good deal."

"He sure did. Do you think Marcus would like guacamole?"

"The avocado would be fine. Not the onions, tomatoes, and hot sauce. I saved him an avocado. Oh, and don't give him a corn chip. He'll choke."

"Gotcha." Setting the squirming boy on the ground, he kept watch as Marcus walked around the kitchen.

Other than the boy's chatter, the room fell silent. Brady set the high chair at the table, placed utensils and plates for him and Amanda, and filled a sippy cup with juice. When the oven timer pinged, he set the bowl of guacamole, chips, and sour cream on the table.

While they ate, she told him about Kelsey showing up. "She paid twice the lesson fee."

"How'd she do?" he asked between bites.

"Better than I expected. She's an accomplished rider. I'd put her on any of our horses."

Swallowing several gulps of water, he set the bottle down. "We are talking about the woman in the red sports car who knows Lance, right?"

"One and the same. She wants another lesson next week. Honestly, I don't know what to offer her. I have what's needed to set up some jumps, which is all I can come up with. When I asked if she'd competed in any events, she shrugged, but didn't give me a real answer."

"Did she tell you anything about her relationship with Lance?" He spooned a small amount of mashed avocado from a bowl, slipping it into Marcus's mouth.

"No, and I didn't ask. She did move into his house."

He popped a chip with guacamole into his mouth, chewing. A minute passed before he spoke. "They must be getting along all right if she moved in."

"He's not there."

Setting down his fork, Brady barked out a laugh.

"I'd like to hear what happens when he returns." She laughed with him. "Kelsey kind of grew on me the longer she was here. She asked if I ever had time to meet for lunch or dinner."

"What did you say?" Brady spooned more mashed avocado into Marcus's mouth.

"She got a call before I could answer."

He finished his second helping of enchilada casserole, setting his fork down. "What would you have told her?"

Pursing her lips, she sat back. "I'd like to meet her for lunch sometime. My guess is Kelsey has a complicated and interesting history. I'd like to hear it."

After putting away the leftovers and cleaning dishes, they moved to the living room. Marcus walked around, exploring anything within his reach. Sitting together after dinner, Amanda hoped Brady would broach the subject that was on both their minds.

Her phone chimed. Pulling it from a pocket, she checked the ID, seeing her sister's name. She showed it to Brady.

"You'd better answer it," he said.

She nodded. "Hello, Tiffany."

"Hey. I've booked my flight. It's a little complicated as there are two stops, then a transfer to the smaller plane, which takes me into Wyoming. I'm so excited. I can't wait to get out there. Mother and Father are angry I'm leaving. I assured them it's another visit. They're afraid I'll move out there to be closer to you."

"Would you, Tiff?"

"Move? Probably not. Right now, I need time away from all the, well...stuff, here at home. I hope you're ready for me."

"Um, yes. What time will you arrive?"

"Tomorrow. Isn't that great!"

Chapter Nineteen

Amanda lay in bed that night, her mind racing as she replayed her sister's phone call. Why hadn't she made up the office when Tiffany first called?

She knew from experience when her sister decided to do something, the excitement would take over, and it would be full steam ahead. Tiffany had two speeds—slow and warp speed.

By not heeding history, Amanda had put herself in a tough position. She already had a full day planned, including a late afternoon final meeting of the Spring Fling Committee. She and Brady had already decided to do the same as always and grab pizza in town. Marcus would join the childcare group, so they'd both be free to participate in the meeting.

What was she going to do with Tiffany? Her sister would arrive anywhere between seven and ten tomorrow night. The odds were good it would be while they were at the meeting.

Well, Tiffany had the door code and knew her way around the house. All Amanda had to do was rise early, make up the sofa bed, clean the desk, and create space in the room's closet. Not too bad.

Having solved the problem, Amanda thought she'd finally go to sleep. It didn't happen.

With her mind clear of Tiffany, it filled with thoughts of Brady. Their relationship had progressed without having the difficult talk she'd envisioned.

Amanda recalled the first time she'd met Mark. She'd been out with friends, having dinner at a restaurant close to the college. A few tables away, Mark sat with friends. She couldn't stop staring at him, glancing away when he looked in her direction.

When her friends were ready to leave, she stayed behind, telling herself it would be for a few minutes, then she'd catch up. Within seconds of them leaving, Mark came to her table, sat down, and introduced himself.

She never did catch up with her friends. And she and Mark had never had a difficult talk about they're relationship. She and Mark had connected, the same as her and Brady.

Letting out a breath, she felt herself relax as the answer came to her. As with Mark, all she had to do was enjoy her time with Brady and let everything else fall into place.

Amanda's alarm beeped much too early. After lying

awake so long, she'd dropped into a deep sleep, not waking once all night. Recalling what needed to be done, she hurried to dress before walking to her late husband's office.

She stopped in the doorway, stunned at the sight before her. The sofa bed was open and made up with sheets, a blanket, large comforter, and pillows. The items on the desk had been organized, and the closet cleared out to make space for Tiffany's clothes.

Whirling around, she rushed down the stairs, slowing when she spotted Brady in the kitchen. He poured her a cup of coffee, adding a little sugar and cream before handing it to her.

Cradling it in her hands, she looked at him. "Thank you."

"No problem." A slow smile curved his lips.

"I mean the office. When did you have time?"

"Early this morning. It didn't take long."

"You should've woken me."

He shrugged. "I knew you were tired. Worried about many things you can't control. It wears you out." Stepping closer, he lifted her chin with a finger. "I know you're scared. So am I."

Finishing his coffee, he set the cup aside. "I'll start the chores. Join me when you're ready."

Brows furrowing, she placed her cup on the table and rushed after him. "Wait, Brady."

"What?"

Standing before him, she met his unwavering gaze. "What are you scared of?"

He ran a finger down her cheek. "You."

Amanda headed out to the barn after dressing and feeding Marcus, wondering if she would find Brady there. Her breath caught when she saw him grooming one of the horses. He turned at the sound of her footsteps, giving her a smile that melted her uncertainty.

Tossing the brush into a plastic caddy, he strode to her. Leaning down, he kissed her before taking Marcus from her arms.

"Good morning, little man," Brady said.

Marcus reached out, patting Brady's cheeks and giggling.

"Did you have breakfast?" Amanda asked.

"Not yet. I want to finish with this horse, then I'll come in. Do you have lessons today?"

"Lance scheduled one. I don't know if he'll show up."

"I'll finish up with the gelding and see you inside." He handed Marcus back to her, returning to the horse.

She stood there watching him, so strong yet so kind. Did he believe what he said about being afraid...of her?

It was at that moment his words made sense.

Returning to the kitchen, she set Marcus down before placing the baby gate in the doorway to the living room. She walked to the window, looking toward the barn where Brady worked.

Grabbing eggs and a package of bacon, she started breakfast. As the bacon fried, Marcus gripped her leg, giggling until she looked down and smiled. Once his mother acknowledged him, he took off toward the back door, then walked to the table.

Keeping an eye on the cooking food and her son, she marveled at how fast he'd gone from a wobbly few steps to running. If she opened the back door, he'd navigate the steps to the ground, then run to the barn in search of Brady.

Absently placing bread in the toaster, she thought about her day. Lance had a lesson mid-morning. She doubted he'd show up. The man was spontaneous, and from her view of the man, unreliable. He jumped from one interest to another, doing whatever felt right at the time.

Whether he showed or not, Tiffany would be driving in sometime in the evening. Whatever was happening in her sister's life, it prompted her to fly across country to spend time at Kicking Horse Ranch. No doubt something had triggered her sister's actions. Knowing Tiffany, she'd spill what bothered her within hours of her arrival.

Which reminded Amanda to call her, let her sister know they may be at the Spring Fling meeting when she arrived. The final meeting before the event the following weekend.

She'd planned all the details for the children's play area, and along with Brady and several others, they'd arrive four hours early to set everything up.

Warmth spread through her at the thought of spending more time with Brady.

Though he lived at the ranch, their schedules took them in different directions each day. She hoped the festival would bring them even closer together.

Brady walked in, stopping all other thoughts. Though Marcus tried to get his attention, his focus was on Amanda. Before she could respond, he closed the distance between them and kissed her tenderly.

"How long before breakfast is ready?"

The quick transition from a surprise, quick kiss to his question stalled her for a moment. "Um...about five minutes."

"Great. I'll wash up, then set the table. Has Marcus eaten?"

"He has, but you know he's going to want some of your eggs."

Stepping over the child's gate, he was on his way to the bathroom when his phone rang. "Hey, Virgil."

"Brady. We're having a ranch meeting at noon tomorrow, and I'd like you to be here."

"I'll be there. What's it about?"

"Jonah and Wyatt want to go over the plans for the guest ranch. Not much longer before the season's first group of visitors arrive."

Brady's mood shifted. Once the season started, all employees were expected to give their complete focus to the ranch. Did this mean he'd no longer be working with Amanda? Would they expect him to move back to Whistle Rock Ranch?

Amanda hummed as she buttoned Marcus's tiny denim overalls. His wide eyes watched her, his chubby fingers grasping at the air. "Mama." She smiled, as she did each time he said her name.

"There we go. You're all ready to go." Amanda picked him up, heading toward the kitchen.

Brady waited by the back door, keys in hand. He grinned when he saw them.

"Hey, little man, lookin' good," he said, ruffling Marcus's hair.

"Badee..." Marcus said.

"Did you hear that? He said my name."

"Badee..." This time, he giggled at the look on Brady's face.

"Yeah, that's right, Marcus." Brady's grin stretched across his face.

She kissed her son's cheek. "Shall we head into town?"

Brady nodded and opened the door for her. The late afternoon sunlight was warm on their skin as they made their way to Brady's truck.

At the pizza parlor, they settled into a booth by the window. Amanda bounced Marcus on her lap while they looked over the menu.

"I wonder why Lance wasn't at the lesson this morning?" Amanda mused after they had ordered.

Brady frowned. "Who knows what goes on with

that guy. We don't even know if he's back in town."

"You're right," Amanda said. "Lance and Kelsey are a mystery."

"He's already paid for the horses and lessons," Brady said.

Amanda nodded, her brow furrowed. Before she could respond, her phone chimed. Pulling it from a pocket, she checked caller ID. Amanda answered.

"Hey, Tiff, what's up?" Her eyes widened at the response. "Whoa, slow down. What happened?"

Brady watched her face as she listened. Her mouth was set in a thin line, her eyes troubled.

"Okay. Take a deep breath. We'll figure this out when you get here," Amanda responded. "See you soon."

She set the phone down and met Brady's questioning gaze. "Tiffany's on her way here from Idaho Falls. Her flights were rerouted. She rented a car and is driving over. She sounds tired and exasperated."

"Where is she?" he asked.

"South of Jackson. She'll be waiting at the ranch for us."

Brady leaned back in the booth, his expression somber. "I'm curious about what brings her back so soon."

Amanda nodded, her eyes distant as she held Marcus. He'd drifted off to sleep in her arms.

Their food arrived, their appetites had diminished after the call. Each wondered what had brought Tiffany back to Brilliance, and what her return might mean.

Finishing their meal, Brady loaded a now wide awake Marcus into his car seat. "We'd better get moving if we want to make that Spring Fling meeting on time." He started the truck and pulled out of the pizza parlor parking lot.

Arriving at the community center, they made their way to the large meeting room. Amanda left for a few minutes to take Marcus to the childcare room. Returning, she spotted Brady at a table with Laurel and Aiden Winters. When Amanda took a seat, Brady grabbed coffees from the refreshment table.

At the front of the room, Mayor Jupiter Jones chatted with Lydia, from Brilliance Coffee & Bakery.

"All right, folks," Mayor Jones called out, tapping the microphone. "This is our last meeting before the festival this weekend. There are still quite a few details to finalize, so let's get started."

The meeting progressed with enthusiastic discussion about vendors, last minute advertising, and activities. Laurel recommended square dancing lessons for kids, which Amanda agreed would be wonderful. Assuming they could find someone to teach.

As the meeting wrapped up, Amanda glanced at her phone. A text from Tiffany.

"At the ranch. All is good. See you guys soon."

Brady noticed the exchange. "Tiffany close?"

Amanda nodded. "She's there." She held up her phone so he could read the text message.

Brady pulled up to the ranch house, spotting Tiffany's rental car. He released Marcus from the car seat and carried him up the porch steps. Amanda was already holding the kitchen door open.

"Tiffany!" Amanda called.

Her sister hurried from the living room, giving Amanda a quick hug. "I made it. And look at you, little man." She tickled Marcus under the chin, eliciting giggles.

"Good to see you, Tiffany," Brady said.

"Thanks," Tiffany said, a bit more subdued.

They entered the living room. While Amanda and Tiffany settled on the sofa, he took a seat in one of the chairs.

"Can I get you anything?" Amanda asked.

Tiffany shook her head, clasping her hands in her lap. "No, I'm okay. Just glad to be here."

Amanda studied her sister. Tiffany's smile seemed strained, her shoulders tense. But before she could inquire further, Tiffany spoke up.

"So tell me about this festival." Her voice held forced enthusiasm. "What do you need help with?"

Amanda glanced at Brady before explaining. "Well, we could use help with the setting up of tents and booths, and the activities in the children's area. I'm sure we'll need extra hands the day of the festival, managing crowds, helping vendors."

"Should be fun." Tiffany nodded, genuine excitement showing on her face and in her voice. "Just tell me when and where. This is exactly what I need."

Brady and Amanda shared a look. What exactly did Tiffany need? For now, they'd make her feel welcome. Anything else could wait.

Chapter Twenty

Brady finished his story about breaking a wild mustang when he was fifteen with a flourish, Amanda and Tiffany laughing so hard they were forced to swipe away tears.

"I didn't know you grew up on a ranch." Tiffany leaned back on the sofa.

"It was my uncle's place. He always needed help with something, and he usually called me. The jobs didn't pay much, but I learned a lot about ranch work." He stood, stretching his arms above his head. "I'm heading to bed. See you two in the morning."

When he'd disappeared down the hall, Tiffany looked at her sister, her eyes glistened with unshed tears. "Thank you," she whispered. "I can't tell you how much being here means."

Amanda reached over and squeezed her hand. "Anytime. That's what family is for." She hesitated. "And when you're ready to talk..."

She nodded, composing herself. "I will. Just...not yet." She rose from the sofa. "I should get to bed, too.

I'm planning to get started with you and Brady."

Amanda walked up the stairs to her own room, her sister's visit foremost on her mind. She'd been right about there being a reason for Tiffany's visit, one her sister wasn't ready to discuss.

Changing into sleeping clothes, she sat on the edge of her bed, tired from another full day. Hearing noises downstairs, she slid into a sweatshirt before walking back downstairs. She stepped into the kitchen to find Brady staring out the window, lost in thought. She studied him for a moment, noting the tension in his shoulders.

"Everything okay?"

He startled, glancing at her with a rueful smile. "Yeah, sorry. I'm thinking about the meeting at Whistle Rock tomorrow."

She slid into a chair. "With Virgil and Wyatt? I thought it was about how the work is going here."

Brady picked up his cup of coffee before taking a seat next to her. She thought it was about Kicking Horse because he'd described the meeting in those terms. "It is. But..." He trailed off, jaw tightening.

"Is there more to it?" When he didn't respond, she leaned forward, lowering her voice. "Brady, talk to me. What's going on?"

He exhaled. "This is a meeting of everyone at the ranch regarding expectations for the upcoming guest ranch season. Sounds like I'm expected to be available, which means I'd need to move back to Whistle Rock."

Her eyes widened as his meaning became clear.

"Everything is going so well."

Reaching out, he covered her hand with his. "I know."

She swallowed, glancing at their hands. "Do you think they expect me to take on all the work here?"

"I'll learn more tomorrow." He lifted his gaze to hers, turmoil in his eyes. "I don't know if I can leave this place. Leave...you."

Amanda's breath caught in her throat at his words. For a moment, neither of them spoke, the weight of his confession hanging between them.

She cleared her throat, careful about her response. "I don't want you to leave, either. I also don't want you to cause trouble between Whistle Rock and my ranch."

Brady nodded, his shoulders slumping. "I agree. The truth is, it's not up to me." He absently stirred the remnants of his coffee.

She squeezed his hand. His eyes met hers, and she offered a small, reassuring smile. "You'll figure it out. And whatever is decided, it won't change what's happening between us."

Brady's expression softened. "You're right. Even if I'm not working or staying here, we'll continue whatever this is." He motioned between the two of them.

Standing, she bent to press a kiss to his lips. "In the meantime, try not to stress too much."

Brady huffed a laugh as he pushed back his chair. "As long as you don't lie awake thinking about what might happen tomorrow."

As they moved toward the hallway, she touched his arm. "It'll work out. I know it will."

He covered her hand with his own, meeting her earnest gaze. "I hope so." With a final squeeze, he headed down the hall, leaving Amanda alone with her swirling thoughts.

She watched his retreating figure, her smile fading. A crease formed between her brows as she mulled over their conversation. The thought of him leaving filled her with an unexpected pang of sadness.

Over the last several weeks, she'd come to rely on Brady's solid presence. His humor and easygoing nature. Not to mention his way with the horses and her students. His absence would leave a hole she had no idea how to fill.

Shaking her head, Amanda walked back up the stairs to her bedroom, heart heavy with the possible ramifications of tomorrow's meeting.

Amanda headed downstairs a little before dawn, thinking of her day. Making a cup of coffee, she poured it into her to-go cup and headed outside. As she made her way toward the stalls, she spotted Brady walking out of the barn.

"Good morning," she called out with a wave and shaky smile.

He lifted his hand. "Morning, Amanda." Opening

his arms, he sighed when she walked into them, wrapping her arms around his waist. "Did you sleep?"

"Some. You?"

"The same." Kissing her temple, he dropped his arms. "I've been up a while. The stock has been fed, and I've checked the automatic waterers. All are working fine."

"Thank you. Seems I don't have anything to do before breakfast."

Brady grinned, his eyes crinkling. "We can fix it together."

They entered the house at the same time Tiffany walked into the kitchen. "Good morning. Have you two already been outside?"

"Yep," Brady answered. "We were going to make breakfast. How does pancakes, eggs, and hashbrowns sound."

"Great. What can I do?"

"Whip up the pancake batter. Your pancakes are always great," Amanda said. She pulled down the ingredients from the cupboard.

"I'll start the hashbrowns," Brady said.

Amanda shot him a grin. "Guess I'll cook the eggs." She'd pulled them from the refrigerator when her baby monitor sounded.

"Do you want me to get him?" Brady asked.

"Sure. He loves seeing you first thing in the morning."

Lowering the heat on the potatoes, Brady took off for Marcus's room. "Hey, little man. I'm coming."

"He's wonderful with Marcus," Tiffany said.

"Brady is great with all children. Marcus loves him, and the feeling is mutual."

Tiffany stopped from measuring the ingredients to look at her sister. "If I didn't know better, I'd think you and Brady are more than friends."

She cracked a few more eggs into a bowl, considering what to say when Brady walked in with Marcus.

"Mama…"

"Hey, sweetheart." She took him from Brady's arms. "Are you hungry?"

Marcus nodded, pointing at the eggs.

"How about scrambled eggs?"

Nodding, he looked at the floor.

"You have to stay in the kitchen if I put you down."

"Doooown…"

Brady whirled around. "Did he just say down?"

She smiled as her son wiggled in her arms. "Yes, I think he did. Down, Marcus?"

He nodded vigorously. "Doooown."

Bending, she lowered him to the floor, then grabbed the gate she used to stop him from wandering into the living room. Securing it in place, she returned to preparing their eggs while keeping an eye on her son.

When the eggs, potatoes, and pancakes were ready, Brady gathered plates and utensils. "How about we fill our plates here instead of putting the food on the table?"

"Works for me," Tiffany answered.

Marcus continued walking around, chattering to

himself, as they sat down. He grabbed his mother's leg when he saw them eating.

"Are you ready to eat?"

"Eeeee…"

Brady lifted him into his high chair and held out a spoonful of eggs. "Here you go."

Tiffany looked between them. "You do know the three of you seem like a real family, right?"

Amanda and Brady looked at each other, then at Tiffany. Neither tried to answer her question. Her insight had jarred them. After a minute, Brady spoke.

"It's something we're talking about, Tiff."

"Really? That's great."

"Tiff, as Brady said, we're figuring stuff out. We may remain good friends, do you understand?"

"Sure. Of course. But if you want my opinion, I think you two are perfect for each other."

Amanda shot a look at Brady, who grinned. "Your sister's right, Tiff. It's too soon to know what will happen."

"Please don't say anything to Mom and Dad," Amanda said. "I can't deal with them right now."

"Don't worry. They're the last people who should know anything about what's going on here." Her voice held a tinge of bitterness neither Brady nor Amanda missed.

"Are they the reason you're here, Tiff?"

She looked at Amanda, but didn't answer. "It's complicated."

"Everything with Mom and Dad are."

The table quieted as they returned to their food,

Brady spooning eggs into Marcus's mouth a little at a time.

Amanda let the familiar rhythm of the horse soothe her as she put the mare through her paces in the arena. Tiffany was in a nearby pasture, exercising another of the horses. This was her personal place, where she felt most at peace.

As she guided the mare into a complicated transition, she spotted Brady in the round pen, working with a four-year-old gelding. Even from her position, his strong, confident presence was evident as he held the lunge line. Brady glanced up and touched the brim of his hat in greeting. Amanda returned the gesture, a mix of emotions welling up.

Slowing the mare, she patted her neck before guiding her horse toward the gate. She wanted to speak with him again before his meeting.

Dismounting, she leaned against the rail, waiting for him to finish. After another minute, he slowed the horse, asked him to stop, then waited for the gelding to face him. A moment later, he swung the gate open and guided the horse out of the round pen.

"He's coming along real nice," she said in approval.

Nodding, he patted the horse's neck. "Yeah, he's a good one. Just needed some focus." He gave her a searching look. "Are you all right?"

Amanda hesitated. "I wanted to make sure you're set for the meeting at Whistle Rock."

His expression grew serious. "Nothing I can do until I hear what Wyatt and Virgil say. Everyone will be there, so I'll wait until the meeting is over to ask about Kicking Horse."

"For what it's worth, I hope you'll stay. You belong here, Brady."

He touched her cheek. "I agree. We'll see what happens." Brady put his hat back on, his eyes shadowed. "I should head over there. It wouldn't be good to be late."

Kissing his cheek, she took a step away. "I'll keep my fingers crossed."

Chapter Twenty-One

Brady's thoughts churned as he drove to Whistle Rock Ranch. He had a lot on his mind, including the insane hours he'd be working during the upcoming guest season, and most of all, Amanda.

Leaving her and Marcus would be harder than he ever imagined. He hadn't told her, but Virgil had made it clear during their phone conversation he needed Brady back at Whistle Rock. Likewise, he hadn't told Virgil about his growing affection for Amanda. He'd never felt so conflicted.

Pulling up to the ranch, he spotted the other hands gathering outside the barn. Getting out of his truck, he felt an unmistakable energy in the air as he approached the group.

Wyatt and Gage were deep in conversation while Jonah was holding a document in his hand, talking to Virgil.

"Hello, Brady," Barrel called out. "Good to have you back."

He nodded, even as his stomach twisted. This

group was like family. Even so, Whistle Rock didn't feel like home anymore. Not without Amanda's bright smile and Marcus's giggles.

He leaned against the barn, listening as the others talked and joked around. But his mind kept wandering back to Kicking Horse Ranch. He'd found a new home there. And leaving it behind for the season would be hard.

Brady was pulled from his thoughts as Virgil stepped onto the back porch, his face unreadable. The chatter died down as everyone focused on the foreman.

"All right, listen up," Virgil bellowed. "We've got a busy summer ahead of us. More guests booked than ever before."

He nodded to Jonah, who consulted his list before speaking. "We're looking at almost full capacity for the last half of June, and all of July, and August. We're over half booked for early June and September."

A murmur rippled through the group. Barrel let out a low whistle. "That's a lot of folks to keep happy."

"You've got that right, Barrel," Virgil said. "And we'll need all hands available this summer. Gage has got the trail rides and activities covered."

Gage stepped forward, arms crossed over his broad chest. "Mornings will be trail rides as usual. I'll also be leading more afternoon fishing trips, as well as overnight camping excursions and rock climbing for the adventurous ones. Oh, and a new option during some of the weeks will be a bus trip to Yellowstone. Those trips will leave early and arrive back here just in time for dinner."

"Can we go?" Barrel asked, getting laughter and clapping in response.

"Some of you will. I'll need one additional person per bus. We're only doing one bus a week, so get your name in early, Barrel." Gage stepped away, with laughter following him.

Brady shifted as unease rushed through him. His gut clenched about the long days and late nights ahead. Thinking about the last couple summers, the guys were definitely ramping things up this year, leaving him little time off.

"Now, I know we're asking a lot," Wyatt said. "You'll be working sunup to sundown on most days. But it's good money. We'll be giving bonuses for extra hours. I know we can count on every one of you to help us make this season a success."

The hands nodded, most of them familiar with how the summer would go. Brady stared down at his boots, anxiety swirling inside him.

How could he leave Amanda? She worked hard and still needed help. The thought of not being there for her, even for an hour or two a couple times a week, twisted his heart.

This would be the hardest summer of his life. What other choice did he have?

The meeting ended after a few more words from Wyatt. The ranch hands dispersed, heading off to attend to their various duties. Brady lingered behind, his mind weighed down by the prospect of the long summer ahead.

"Hey, Brady, got a minute?" Virgil approached, his brows drawn together in a frown.

"Sure, what's up?"

Virgil motioned for Brady to walk with him. They headed toward one of the empty corrals.

"I know this summer won't be easy for anyone," Virgil said. "Especially for you."

Brady nodded, waiting for his cousin to continue.

"Now, I don't claim to know everything going on between you and Amanda," Virgil said, his voice softening. "But I've got eyes and real good ears."

Brady felt his cheeks grow warm. Were he and Amanda that obvious?

"Point is, I know you care about her. And that ranch of hers needs our help."

"Yeah, it does," he nodded. Thinking about not being there to help Amanda made his chest ache.

Virgil stopped walking and turned to Brady, his wise eyes searching the younger man's face.

"I know you want to be there for Amanda. The truth is, we need you here. I wish things were different, but they're not."

Brady swallowed hard. "I know. It's just..."

"You don't have to explain," Virgil said, holding up a hand. "Believe me, I understand. I spoke with Wyatt, and we've got a plan."

"What kind of plan?"

"Lucas Kovak."

"The Navy SEAL guy? The one who knows Deputy

Winters?"

Virgil nodded. "Yep. I talked to Lucas last week and hired him on the spot. The sheriff has offered him a job as soon as a deputy position opens up. He needed something temporary until then. He's got ranch experience. Grew up on a ranch in Texas. I'm sending him over to help Amanda while you're here with us."

Brady considered this, not sure how he felt about a single, good-looking guy working with Amanda. Still, having an experienced ranch hand helping out at Kicking Horse was the priority.

"Are you sure he's the right man?" Brady asked.

"I already spoke with him. He'll head over to Kicking Horse tomorrow morning," Virgil assured him.

Brady let out a long breath, feeling a huge sense of relief. Amanda would have help. The ranch would survive the summer. He could be here, where the Whistle Rock crew needed him most, and visit when he had time.

"Virgil, I...I don't know what to say," Brady stammered.

He clasped Brady's shoulder. "You don't need to say anything. Let's give this guest season everything we've got. When it's over, you can head back to Kicking Horse. What do you say?"

Brady met Virgil's eyes and nodded, relief and resolve flooding through him.

"I'm in."

Brady drove back to Kicking Horse Ranch, thinking over what Virgil had arranged. Lucas helping Amanda was the perfect solution, even as his stomach roiled at the thought of leaving her and Marcus.

Amanda carried Marcus outside as he pulled up to the ranch house. Brady climbed out, his boots crunching on the gravel as he walked to them.

"Hey," she said with her usual smile. "How'd the meeting go?" He could hear the tension in her voice.

Hesitating, he forced a smile. "Overall, it was good. There's something I need to talk to you about."

Amanda's brow furrowed slightly. "What is it?"

Brady took a breath. "Virgil wants me back at Whistle Rock for the summer. It's, uh..." he released a heavy breath, "not negotiable."

Her face fell. She handed Marcus into Brady's outstretched hands. "It's not a surprise."

"The season is almost booked to capacity. Virgil really needs me there."

"No, you should go. I know how much the Bonners and Virgil rely on you."

"I feel awful about leaving you and Marcus."

She offered an understanding smile. "We'll manage, somehow. This ranch has seen tough times before."

"There's some good news. Virgil's sending someone to help out here until I can come back. Do you remember Lucas Kovak?"

She looked surprised. "The Navy SEAL? Winters' friend?"

"That's the one. He left the Navy and is waiting for a deputy position to open up. He was raised on a ranch in Texas, so he's got good experience."

"Well, that's good to hear," Amanda said, relief evident in her voice. "Not as good as having you here, though."

Nodding, he held her gaze. "I'll come by whenever I can get away."

"We'd like that."

They stood in silence for a moment, the weight of Brady's impending departure hanging over them.

After a minute, he stepped forward and pulled Amanda into an embrace with Marcus nestled between them. She wrapped her free arm around his back, holding him against her.

"Thank you," she whispered. "For everything."

He nodded, overcome with emotion. After a long moment, they pulled apart.

Brady cleared his throat. "Have you eaten?"

"Tiffany's getting it ready."

"Great, 'cause I'm starving."

He turned toward the house, heart heavy. Tomorrow, he'd leave this place, and the woman and child who'd come to mean so much to him.

Brady packed up his meager belongings early the next morning. He folded his shirts and jeans, and gathered his toiletries from the bathroom, placing everything neatly into a duffel bag and backpack.

It was a heartrending feeling to pack up and leave the place he now considered home. He'd miss the peacefulness and natural beauty of the ranch. Most of all, he'd miss Amanda and Marcus, who'd filled a void in his life he hadn't even realized existed.

He took one last look around the sparse bedroom. He'd hold onto the memories made here until his return when the summer season ended. The change was inevitable, as was his duty to return to Whistle Rock.

Tossing his bags into his truck, he walked back into the house as Amanda entered the kitchen. Dressed in jeans and a flannel shirt, she was ready for another day of work. A day without him working horses in a nearby pasture. She offered a brave smile.

"Good morning," she said. "So, you have time for breakfast?"

He shook his head. "I'd better head over."

They stood facing each other, neither knowing quite what to say. She broke the silence. "Drive safe, okay? You know where we are whenever you have some free time."

Brady nodded, his throat tight. He forced a tight grin. "You haven't gotten rid of me, Amanda. I'm only fifteen minutes away. I'll come visit as often as I can."

"I know you will." She stepped forward, embracing him, her arms tightening around him. He breathed in the faint scent of her shampoo, memorizing the feel of her in his arms.

After a long moment, they pulled back. Brady cleared his throat. "I'd better hit the road."

With a heavy heart, he turned and walked to his truck. As he pulled away, watching Amanda wave at him from the porch, he returned the wave as the ranch disappeared from view.

Brady drove in silence, a mix of emotions assaulting him. Logically, he knew they'd be separated by a short distance, not hundreds of miles or days away. It seemed silly to be bothered by the turn of events.

The reality was, he felt as if his world had been upended. He'd be putting in fourteen to sixteen hours of work each day before falling into bed. There would be times he'd work straight through from one week to another with no days off.

Before now, he'd thrived on the schedule. The Bonners were generous with the bonus pay to each ranch hand. The money was worth more than double or triple time pay. After spending his evenings with Marcus and Amanda, his priorities had changed. Though the few months away would pass quickly, he'd rather be at Kicking Horse.

And if he were honest with himself, he knew his feelings for Amanda ran much deeper than friendship. There had always been an undeniable connection between them, though neither had acted upon it. Leaving now left those possibilities unexplored.

Brady gripped the steering wheel tighter. He knew

this was the right choice. Virgil needed him at Whistle Rock.

His heart didn't care about what he should and shouldn't do. It wanted what it wanted—more time with Amanda, watching Marcus grow. Maybe even a chance for marriage and a family of his own.

With a deep sigh, Brady turned onto the highway toward Whistle Rock Ranch. The familiar road unwound before him, but it felt different now. He was different. Living with Amanda and Marcus had changed him in ways he was still figuring out.

As Whistle Rock came into view, Brady braced himself. This was for the best, he reminded himself.

Parking his truck, Brady stepped out, grabbed his bags, and headed toward the bunkhouse. Ranch hands called out greetings, welcoming him back. Inside, the familiar smell of leather and hard work surrounded him.

Virgil appeared in the doorway, breaking into a wide grin. "You're here early. Beth and Abbie are just setting out breakfast. Come on, I'll walk over with you."

Brady forced a smile as he kept pace with Virgil on the way into the lodge. The aromas of cooked ham and bacon assaulted him. He'd almost forgotten the amount of food available early each morning.

Looking around the dining area, he spotted all the familiar faces. A chorus of greetings rose up as they noticed Brady. He nodded in return, moving to fill a plate and grab a seat.

Digging into the meal, he studied the ranch hands

around him. These were his closest friends, people who meant a great deal to him. Another type of family from the one he already missed at Kicking Horse.

This had been the right choice, hadn't it? He tuned out the chatter around him, lost in his own conflicted thoughts.

Chapter Twenty-Two

"You all right, Brady?" Wyatt asked, nudging his shoulder.

Brady blinked, realizing he'd been staring into an empty corral. "Yeah. Guess I was daydreaming."

Clasping his shoulder, Wyatt looked past the corral to the pasture where horses grazed. "I hear you. Must be a real transition from a ranch with two people working the stock to returning to Whistle Rock."

"I'd forgotten the amount of activity around here. It's all good, though. Both ranches are where they should be."

"That's what I wanted to talk to you about."

Brady turned to face him. "About what?"

"How is it going over there? Are you and Amanda keeping up with the work?"

"For now, yes. All six mares will drop foals in the spring. By the second spring, she'll need more than one ranch hand. She's a real hard worker, Wyatt. She keeps up with me just fine. I sold two of her horses a week back. There's never a lull in work over there."

"Good to hear. Lucas Kovak is packing to drive to Kicking Horse. He's in the bunkhouse. Do you mind talking to him before he leaves?"

"Nope. I'll do that now."

Brady entered the bunkhouse, unsure of what to say to the man who'd be taking his place for the next several months. A knot formed in his throat when he spotted Lucas at his bunk, closing up a duffle similar to his own. His sandy blond hair was a little longer, but it was the same man he'd met several months earlier.

"Hey, Lucas." He walked toward him.

"Brady." He held out his hand. "Good to see you."

Grasping it, Brady nodded. "Thought you might want to talk a minute before heading to Kicking Horse Ranch."

"Sure thing. Sit down and tell me what I need to know."

They spoke for thirty minutes about what Brady had been doing, and the plans for the future of the ranch. Then he talked about Amanda, Marcus, and the visiting sister, Tiffany.

"That's about it."

Lucas's lips quirked up at the corners. "How long have you been in love with Amanda?"

Brady startled at the knowing look in Lucas's eyes. "I, uh..." He grinned back at Lucas. "Is it that obvious?"

"I can't speak for anyone else, but it's pretty clear to me. Does she know?"

"I've never told her outright. Pretty sure she knows, though."

"Do you mind a suggestion?"

Brady nodded.

"Tell her. Women like to hear the words." Standing, Lucas slid on his sunglasses and grabbed his duffle. He held out his hand. "Thanks for the information."

Standing, Brady clasped Lucas's hand. "Watch over them for me."

"Count on it."

The sound of an engine pulled Amanda from her work. A white truck came up the drive, and she watched as a tall, muscular man with collar-length blond hair stepped out. His startling blue eyes locked on hers.

"Hello, Amanda. It has been a while." Lucas walked over to offer his hand. "Good to meet you."

"Same here. I understand you took a temporary job at Whistle Rock."

"You heard right. Sheriff Duggan offered me a job as soon as the city council approves the position. It means they also have to approve an expanded budget. If they don't, I'll wait until one of the deputies leave."

"So now you're a ranch hand."

"Again." He chuckled.

She laughed. "Brady called while you were driving over. He said you grew up on a ranch in Texas. He, uh…told me to ignore your ugly face and short stature, and give you a chance."

A bark of laughter broke from deep in Lucas's throat. "He did, huh? Well, I'll have to find some way of paying him back for the kind words."

"So, what do you want to do first? Get settled or look around?"

"Look around if you have time."

"Time is all I have. Come on." She started walking to the barn where the stallions had their stalls when the porch door slammed. Glancing over her shoulder, she saw Tiffany hurry down the steps.

"Tiff, come over and meet our new ranch hand."

Her sister rushed toward them, holding out her hand. "Tiffany Aldrich, Amanda's sister."

He gently grasped her hand. "Lucas Kovak. Nice to meet you."

"So, you're the one taking Brady's place?"

"For a few months. Brady will be back as soon as Virgil releases him." His chuckle caused the women to grin.

"I was going to show him around. Do you want to come with us, Tiff?"

"Sure. Lucia's inside, so I was coming out to help anyway."

"Lucia?" Lucas asked.

"She watches my young son, Marcus, five days a week. Her husband drops her off in the morning, and

Bra...um, I drive her back to town after Marcus goes down for his afternoon nap."

"Ah..."

"I can do that as long as I'm here, Amanda," Tiffany said.

"Perfect. Okay, this is the stud barn. We have two Morgan stallions for breeding our six Morgan mares. All will drop foals next spring."

"Virgil mentioned a partnership with Whistle Rock," Lucas said.

"Kicking Horse and the Bonners are partnering to breed and sell Morgans. They hope the program will be as successful as the horse breeding program at Whistle Rock. Obviously, I hope the same. Here they are. Ceasar and Hannibal."

"Those are two magnificent stallions. Any idea what the Bonners paid for them?" Lucas asked.

Amanda mentioned a price. "It's far more than I could ever do on my own. Plus, they purchased the mares. Anson Bonner got them through a friend of his."

"I've heard Anson is well-connected." Lucas walked closer, knowing how unpleasant some stallions could be. "How's their disposition?"

"Better than I expected. Brady has ridden both of them."

"Can I ride one?" Tiffany asked.

Amanda glared at her. "No."

Tiffany crossed her arms. "I'm an excellent rider."

"I know you are. Those stallions aren't the same as the horses you ride back home. Ceasar and

Hannibal haven't been ridden much. They're temperamental and hard to handle."

"Excuse me, but Amanda is right," Lucas said.

Arms still crossed, Tiffany pinned him with an icy look. "Can you ride them?"

He shrugged. "Probably."

When Tiffany didn't respond, Amanda walked between them. "Time to show you the mares."

Tiffany set the lasagna on the counter, next to the salad and warm bread, as Lucas walked into the kitchen from finishing his late afternoon chores.

"Something smells great. Lasagna? Did you make it?"

Tiffany felt her face heat. "Yes. It's our grandmother's recipe. Amanda and I have been making it since we were teenagers." She looked down at his boots, then back up to meet his gaze. "The mud room is behind you. There's a sink, and you can leave your boots on the rack. Oh, and there's a door from the porch directly into it."

Her slight rebuke didn't bother him. He'd been dressed down by the best and survived. "Thanks. I'll go wash up."

"Are you going to help with the Spring Fling Festival this weekend?" Tiffany set the food on the kitchen table.

"Of course he is." Amanda walked into the kitchen with Marcus trailing behind her.

"I am?" Lucas joined them.

"Everyone goes to the festival. I'm certain Laurel and Aiden will be there." Amanda mentioned Lucas's friends. "Sheriff Duggan and some of his deputies are always on site, too."

"Brady and Amanda are in charge of the children's game area. I'm going to help, too."

"We could use another person, Lucas. Oh, and Brady is helping at the chili cookoff."

"Now you're talking my language. I'll help out."

"It'll mean getting the chores done early. We should be at the park by seven-thirty," Amanda told Lucas.

"No problem."

Tiffany glanced between them. "All right. Dinner's on the table."

Chapter Twenty-Three

Tiffany closed the back door behind her, stopping on the porch for a few minutes to clear her head. A long walk might help her sort out what she'd heard before leaving Vermont, and how to explain it all to Amanda.

She wished Brady still worked at Kicking Horse. His presence would've calmed Amanda when she heard what Tiffany had to say.

"But he's not here," she muttered as she passed the stud barn on her walk.

"Hey, Tiffany. Where are you going?"

Her sister's voice had her turning around. Amanda stood at the porch rail, watching her. Knowing her time to decide what she'd say was up, she walked back to the house.

"I needed to get out for a bit," Tiffany explained as she joined her sister on the porch.

"It is a beautiful evening. Mark and I used to walk when the weather permitted. He always had to check on the stock one more time before going to bed."

"You still miss him."

Amanda nodded. "I think about him every day. Mostly, I wish he'd been alive to see his son."

"He would've been proud of what you've accomplished in the last two years."

"Do you think so, Tiff?"

"I know so." She draped an arm over Amanda's shoulders. "Let's go inside. There's something I need to tell you."

"Will I like it?"

Tiffany chuckled. "Probably not."

Inside, Amanda fixed cups of tea, setting them on the table. "All right. I'm ready."

Drawing the cup toward her, Tiffany took a sip. "This is good. What is it?"

"I don't know. Laurel at Florals & Floats gave it to me."

"I love it." She took another sip, searching for the right words.

"Whatever you have to say, spill it, Tiff. This waiting is making me crazy."

Shifting in her chair, she opened her mouth, then closed it. Meeting Amanda's worried gaze, she took a breath. "Our parents have been talking to Mark's parents about you."

Her brows drew together. "Me?"

"And Marcus. I don't know how often the four of them talk, but I've heard them three times."

"What are they saying?"

Tiffany paused, her heart pounding. She knew the second she told Amanda about her parents' plans, there'd be no going back. Amanda would be devastated, furious even. Tiffany knew keeping this from her would be far worse.

"They're making plans about you, and the ranch."

Amanda stiffened. "What kind of plans?"

"They don't think you can handle this place on your own. Not with a baby to care for. They want to somehow force you to sell the ranch and either return to Vermont or move close to Mark's parents in Idaho."

Amanda shot to her feet, hands balled into fists. "They want to take my home away from me? My land? My son?" Her voice shook with fury.

"What's going on in here?"

"Brady!" Amanda ran into his open arms. "They're trying to take Marcus away from me."

Kissing her forehead, he looked at Tiffany. "Is that so?"

She offered a helpless nod. "They're worried about you and Marcus. Even so, I couldn't let them make those choices for you."

Amanda muttered something under her breath, moving out of Brady's arms. "Well, it's not going to happen." She closed the distance between her and her sister, eyes blazing. "I won't let them do this. I don't care what they think is best. This is my land, my ranch. I decide what happens here."

"Everything all right in here?" Lucas walked in from the living room, sending a quick chin lift to Brady.

Amanda sighed, raking a hand through her hair.

"No, everything is not okay." She explained the situation, watching Lucas's expression darken. He looked at Brady, who shook his head.

"Sit down, Amanda," Brady said in a calm voice. "Listen, we won't let them take this place from you. They aren't going to do anything you don't want."

She searched his face. "You're sure?"

"The ranch belongs to you. The deed is in your name."

She looked at Tiffany. "Do you think they'll try to take Marcus?"

"I believe they'll try scaring you into thinking they will. Brady is right. The ranch is yours, and Marcus is your son. What they're discussing is, well..."

"Unconscionable," Lucas said.

Tiffany looked at him. "Right."

"Everyone around here knows you're a great mother," Brady said. "They'd have a hard time proving you aren't."

"As I said, our parents want you to move back east and find someone who will take care of you and Marcus. Mark's parents want the same, except for you to move close to them in Idaho. The four of them have this idea you need someone to take care of you."

Amanda shook her head. "I can take care of myself."

"I know you can, sis. Remember, neither Mark's mother nor ours ever worked outside the home. They've never held a paying job or been responsible for paying the bills. And we had a nanny so Mom could do her social stuff. They don't understand how capable you are."

"Or how important it is for me to carry on Mark's dream." Amanda shot a look at Brady, who covered her hand with his. He looked at Tiffany.

"When are they planning to come out here?"

"I don't know, but soon."

Amanda jumped up and walked to the kitchen window. Her jaw clenched as she looked out at the land and buildings making up Kicking Horse Ranch. She'd worked alongside Mark, and now Brady, to turn a profit. Tiffany was right when she reminded her their mother knew nothing about the struggles she'd faced, or how far she'd come since Mark died. Whirling around to face the others, she released an angry breath.

"They will not take away either the ranch or Marcus," she fumed. "I may be a single mother, but I'm quite capable of working and being a mother."

"That's all good, Amanda," Lucas said. "I know this isn't my business, but my sense is you need something more than to tell them you're capable. They probably already know they can't take Marcus away or force you to sell the ranch. The problem is you'll spend time worrying and arguing and taking time away from what you want to be doing. You need something strong enough to make both sets of parents back off. Something they can't do anything about."

"They'll have nowhere to go..." Brady muttered.

Lucas pointed at him. "Exactly."

Amanda leaned against the counter, staring down

at her boots. "What would that be?"

Brady stood, glancing between Lucas and Tiffany. "Do you two mind giving Amanda and me a few minutes?"

Lucas shoved back his chair to stand. "Not at all."

"Fine with me," Tiffany said. She followed Lucas into the living room.

When they were gone, Brady took Amanda's hand. "Let's walk out on the porch, okay?"

Nodding, they stepped out the back door to the railing. Looking up at the clear sky, neither of them spoke for a full minute.

"What am I going to do, Brady? Lucas is right. I need something so conclusive, they'll stop whatever they have planned."

Squeezing her hand, he turned her to face him. "I may have a simple solution to the problem."

"A simple solution?"

"Yeah."

"That would be wonderful, Brady. What is it?"

"Marry me."

Amanda stared at him in shock. "What?"

"Marry me," Brady repeated. "There will be nothing they can do if we're married."

Her mind whirled. Marry Brady? Could it work? She cared about him a great deal, maybe loved him. Was her love strong enough to make a marriage work?

"I love you, Amanda. Have for a long time." He grasped her other hand. "Marcus is like my own son."

"You'd make a wonderful father, Brady. Marcus

loves you."

"What about you?" He continued to hold her hands. "Do you think you could ever love me?"

For the last two years, he'd been her rock, a man she could depend on, who gave up his free time to be with her and Marcus. He was kind and humble, someone she never tired of being around. Brady had also been the friend Mark trusted most.

Looking into his steady, dark gray eyes, she knew in her heart how she felt about him. "I already love you."

Chapter Twenty-Four

Brady pulled her close. "You're sure?"

"I couldn't be more sure."

Lifting her into the air, he spun around, hearing the joyous sound of her laughter. Setting her down, his mouth covered hers. He deepened the kiss before raising his head to look into her deep blue eyes. "We've got this, sweetheart. I promise you, we've got this. Let's tell Tiffany and Lucas."

He settled an arm over her shoulders, turning her toward the door.

"Wait."

"Yes?"

"What are you thinking? I mean, about getting married."

"Soon."

She glanced at him, then laughed. Entering the house, she slowed. "I know I'm sure about this. Are *you* certain this is what you want, Brady?"

"Amanda, I've never wanted anything as much as I want to be your husband and Marcus's father." He brushed a quick kiss across her lips. "Let's tell them."

"All right. Be aware, Tiffany is going to want to plan the wedding."

"As long as it happens soon, I don't care who plans it."

Guiding her to the living room, they found Lucas and Tiffany playing cards. "Gin!" she called out, spotting them.

"She's killing me," Lucas said.

"She's a gin shark." Amanda chuckled. "I should've warned you."

"No worries. We're going bowling next week. I'll get revenge then." He noticed something in Brady's expression. "What's going on?"

"Do you want to tell them?" Brady asked.

"No, you go ahead."

"I asked Amanda to marry me..."

"What?" Tiffany almost screamed.

"And," Brady continued, "she said yes."

Jumping up, Tiffany ran to her sister, embracing her. "Oh, my gosh. I'm so happy for you." Turning, she hugged Brady. "This is the best news I've heard in a long time."

"Congratulations, bro," Lucas said, shaking Brady's hand. "I'm real happy for you." He turned to hug Amanda, then looked back at Brady. "You're a lucky man."

"Don't I know it."

"When?" Tiffany bounced on the balls of her feet in excitement.

Before Amanda could answer, Brady responded.

"Soon. Tomorrow, if we can arrange it."

Tiffany's enthusiasm faded. "So soon?"

Lucas nodded. "Brilliant idea. If you're going to marry, do it before the parents get to town."

Hearing this, Tiffany brightened. "Of course. Okay. I'll make coffee, and we can get this marriage figured out."

Brady had returned to Whistle Rock after midnight, tired and exhilarated. He couldn't quite believe Amanda had agreed to be his wife. Unlike some families Brady knew, he and Amanda would be true partners, working together to make the ranch prosper.

Stepping into a cool morning, he saw Wyatt and Virgil talking outside the barn. He and Amanda had agreed to keep the wedding small. Very, very small.

Tiffany had volunteered to take on several tasks to make the wedding happen in a short period of time. She'd also recruited Lucas to help her, leaving the engaged couple to focus on the important items—obtaining a license, buying rings, and deciding what to wear.

Neither Amanda nor Brady owned a large selection of clothes. He'd wear a new pair of jeans, a white long-sleeved shirt, a bolo neck tie his parents had gifted him on his eighteenth birthday, black boots, and a new Stetson straw cowboy hat.

After hearing what Brady planned, Amanda decided to wear a cream colored, lace-up the front, sleeveless jacquard swing dress. Her Lucchese blue, turquoise, and sea green boots would work well with it, as would her light-colored Stetson with blue and sea green hat band. Both had been a gift from Tiffany the Christmas before Mark died.

Those decided, all the couple had to do was decide on rings and obtain the license. Brady and Amanda would meet in town in a few hours with the hope of finalizing both.

Watching as Wyatt and Virgil parted, he followed his cousin into the barn. "Hey, Virg."

The foreman turned, a smile forming. "Heard you came back late."

"Later than I'd planned. I need to speak with you alone."

The smile fading, he motioned for them to go into the large tack room. "This work?"

Brady nodded, feeling a distinct wave of nerves settling in his stomach. "It's about Amanda...and me."

"All right."

"I asked her to marry me. She accepted."

Not much shocked Virgil. By the way his features slackened while his eyes grew wide, Brady knew his cousin hadn't expected this.

"Are you sure this is what you want?"

"Yes."

"Then I'm glad for you. When will you marry?"

"The day after tomorrow, assuming we can get a license and rings by then."

Virgil's composed expression cracked when he laughed. "You're not kidding, are you?"

"No. There are reasons why, which I'll explain when there's time."

Crossing his arms, Virgil leaned against a stall. "I have time now."

Twenty minutes later, they walked out of the tack room with Virgil agreeing to be at the wedding with his wife, Lily. As they stepped into the morning sun, he turned to Brady.

"Be sure you aren't doing this to help Amanda. Marriage isn't easy. If you aren't genuinely in love with each other, the union won't work."

"I'd already planned to ask her. The issue with Marcus's grandparents made it more urgent."

Virgil drew him into a hug. "I will always have your back, Brady."

"And I will have yours."

Per Virgil's suggestion, Brady left the ranch after lunch. Instead of meeting Amanda in town, he drove to her ranch, finding the three of them working outside. Lucas was in the round pen, Tiffany in another, and Amanda stood in the arena, watching Lance make figure eights on Chance.

At least the man had shown up. Brady wondered what ever happened with him and his friend, Kelsey Kinneman. Well, it wasn't his business, nor did he care.

She'd flashed him a brilliant smile and waved when spotting his truck coming up the drive.

Climbing out, he stopped when his phone chimed. "Yeah?"

"Brady?"

His stomach clenched when he recognized the voice. He wondered what the Bonner matriarch wanted. "It's me. What can I do for you?"

"This is Margie Bonner. Maybe I should talk to you and Amanda at the same time."

"Talk to me and we'll call back if needed."

"All right. Almost everything is set. The clerk at city hall can see you at four today, Jayson's Jewelers expects you at five. Now, Janel and Micah know you're on a budget, so they aren't going to push any of their expensive rings on you two. Laurel Winters expects you at six to select flowers for Amanda's bouquet. Lydia at Brilliance Coffee & Bakery has agreed to make your wedding cake. We could have the wedding here at Whistle Rock, but Amanda would probably prefer it at Kicking Horse. Pastor Ellison can perform the ceremony tomorrow at one o'clock. Will that work?"

"Uh..."

"Since it's his only opening, we'll make it work. People will have eaten lunch, and it will be too early for dinner, so it's light appetizers, cake, cookies, brownies, coffee, tea, soda, and beer. Beth and Abigail are already working on the appetizers, cookies, and brownies. Oh, and champagne, of course. Anson and I will bring plenty with us. Can't have a wedding without champagne." She laughed. "Cups, glasses, forks, spoons, and the rest have already been set aside. Do you and Amanda know what you're wearing?"

"Yes, ma'am."

"Excellent. Daisy is passing the word around to a few people. We understand this is a small wedding. Any questions?"

"No, ma'am."

"Great. Have Amanda call me when she's available." Margie ended the call.

"Yes, ma'am," he whispered, wondering what had just happened.

The four of them sat on the back porch after dinner, watching Marcus run around. Brady and Amanda had decided on simple platinum bands for their rings. Micah Jayson had engraved them without an extra charge, and Janel Jayson gave Amanda a boxed silver charm. The thoughtfulness of two people she barely knew had her eyes tearing.

Brady had recounted Margie's phone call several times as Amanda, Tiffany, and Lucas laughed. He'd fallen in love with the perfect woman. Amanda hadn't minded Margie jumping in to organize tomorrow's wedding.

"The woman is a saint," she'd said with a smile.

"I don't believe I've met her, but she sounds amazing." Tiffany chuckled.

"She is that, and more," Brady said.

"This is going to be a crazy couple days for you two." Lucas took a long swallow from his bottle of water. "Getting married tomorrow and the Spring Festival on Saturday. Which reminds me. Where will you be staying tomorrow night?"

Brady lowered his head, chuckling. "Margie called back to say she'd booked us a room at Brilliance Inn B&B. She made it for two nights, but Amanda called and changed it to one night."

"It's too bad we have to get up so early Saturday for the festival. I'd love to enjoy the B&B another night." Amanda's voice held a bit of wistfulness.

"We'll do it again sometime, sweetheart." Taking her hand, Brady looked up to see a shooting star, and made a wish.

Amanda pulled the dress over her head, feeling the material brush against her calves as it settled on her shoulders. Looking in the mirror, she straightened the straps and stared.

She hadn't taken much time to consider what the marriage to Brady would mean for her and Marcus. Taking a breath, she released it, considering the changes. After a few minutes, a slow grin spread across her face. Whatever changes came with their marriage, they'd be for the best.

Hearing the sound of an approaching vehicle, she looked out the window. A large SUV was parked near the barn. Six people exited. Anson and Margie Bonner, Wyatt and Daisy Bonner, and Virgil and Lily Redcloud. Her heart warmed, knowing they cared enough to attend.

Checking the time, she hurried to finish dressing. She looked up when she heard a knock on the bedroom door a second before Tiffany joined her. She stopped to stare at her sister.

"You look gorgeous. Brady's going to swallow his tongue."

Amanda burst out laughing. It was what they used to say when they were teenagers. She couldn't remember the last time she'd heard it.

"Everything is almost ready downstairs. Pastor Ellison just arrived. Brady is walking around, greeting everyone. He isn't as shy as I remembered."

"He's more outgoing around people he knows." Amanda finished putting on earrings, and took one more look in the mirror. "This is as good as it's going to get."

Tiffany touched her arm. "You truly are beautiful. Ready to become Mrs. Blackwolf?"

"Yes, I am."

Walking down the stairs, she stopped at the sound of laughter, and people talking. Not the sound of a few close friends. What she heard had her slowing as they reached the last step.

Looking out the back door, her throat tightened. She turned to face Tiffany. "How many people are out there?"

"I don't know for certain."

"Guess."

"About a hundred." Tiffany shrugged, her mouth twisting. "Seems word got out."

"It was supposed to be a small wedding." She continued watching as another truck arrived with five more people. When the back door opened, she jolted, then relaxed when Brady walked inside.

"Wow. You are...just...wow."

Smiling, she moved closer, reaching for his hand.

Chapter Twenty-Five

Brady and Lucas strained to place the mechanical bull in the children's area of the festival. "We should've spent the money to have them place this thing," Brady huffed out.

"Tell me again why you didn't?" Lucas adjusted the piece of machinery on the mat they were using to slide the bull into position.

"It was a last minute idea." Brady drew in a breath. "We didn't have it budgeted."

"Ah, gotcha. Next time, I'll write a check to cover it."

Brady blew out a laugh. "It wouldn't have been quite so hard if Lance had shown up. Somehow, I knew that guy would bail on us."

"The bull looks great." Amanda stood several feet away. "It is quite a bit smaller than the one for adults. Perfect for the children."

"Right." Lucas released a heavy breath. "What's next?"

"Everything's in place," Amanda said. "The bull

was the last job before they open the festival in a few minutes. It's going to be great."

Though exhausted from their wedding day, she felt energized and ready to see the results of the committee's work.

Feeling Brady's approach, she turned to accept the kiss he offered. "I love you, Amanda."

"And I love you."

A siren rang twice, signaling the festival's opening. "Guess this is it," Lucas said. "I'm going to look for Tiffany to see if I can help with anything else. Call me if there's anything else I can do around here."

"Thanks, Lucas," she called after him, seeing his hand raise in a wave as the first children entered the play area.

"Anyone hungry?" Tiffany walked toward Amanda and Brady carrying two large bags. "Lucas is helping a vendor secure his pop-up." She looked at Brady. "He told me to tell you not to eat too much if you want to power down at the chili cookoff."

"I could eat half a beef and still be hungry for chili. What's in the bags?"

"Sandwiches, chips, drinks, cookies. The usual festival fare. Hey, Amanda. Are you going to eat?" Tiffany set the food on a table in the back.

"Go ahead. I need to watch the children."

"I'll talk to her," Brady said. "All the children have at least one parent with them. All we've done is watch."

Tiffany glanced past him, then froze. "Oh, no."

"What?" Brady asked.

"See those four people standing outside the temporary fence?"

He nodded. "I recognize your parents, Peggy and Reginald Aldrich. The others are Mark's parents. I saw them at his funeral service."

"I was hoping you and Amanda wouldn't have to deal with them this soon."

"It's better to get it over with early, Tiff."

"Well, there's no putting it off now. Amanda is talking with Mom and Dad."

"I'd better join my bride."

"You set them straight, Brady," Tiff yelled as he jogged through the play area, dodging children and parents.

Slowing to a walk, he pasted on a smile as he stopped beside Amanda. Leaning over, he kissed her cheek.

"Mr. and Mrs. Aldrich. Good to see you again. You also, Mr. and Mrs. Swanson." He held out a hand to both sets of parents, pulling it back to drape over Amanda's shoulders when no one responded. "Have you told them the good news, sweetheart?"

"I was just about to."

"What news?" Peggy asked.

Instead of answering, she held up her left hand. The single diamond, yellow-gold engagement ring and wedding ring had been replaced with a simple platinum band.

"Is that?" Her mother gasped. "What have you done?"

"Brady and I are married."

"No," Mark's parents said in unison.

She glanced between the two couples. "I'm sorry if this comes as a shock. We fell in love, and Marcus is crazy about Brady." Amanda leaned into him. "So am I."

Amanda moved her gaze from her parents to her former in-laws. "How about we all meet for dinner tonight at the house? Brady and I will pick up something on our way home."

"That may be best," Reginald said. "We'll take care of the food, though. When will you get home?"

"The afternoon volunteers will be here by three, so we should be there by four," Amanda replied.

"All right. We'll see you then." Though her mother's voice had calmed, her expression warned them the worst was yet to come.

Brady pulled off the main road onto the ranch's drive. "Are you ready for this, sweetheart?"

"I keep telling myself there's nothing they can do, and to stay calm."

"They're your parents, which means they'll always

worry about you. You'll do the same with Marcus."

"I hope I'll give him space to make his own choices. Looks like Dad is waiting for us on the porch. Here goes." Amanda steeled herself for the confrontation to come.

Parking, Brady walked around the truck to open the passenger door, helping her out. They held hands as they walked up the steps.

"Right on time," her father said. "Your mother has dinner already set out." He held the back door open for them. "Is your sister coming?"

Amanda shook her head. "No. Tiff's staying at the festival. She's sort of a roving volunteer, helping out where needed."

"Sounds like our Tiffany."

Brady squeezed her hand, then let go as they entered the kitchen. The women were talking together near the sink.

"Took you long enough to get here," her mother bit out. "The food's almost cold."

Amanda walked to the table, checking the dishes they'd bought. Picking up one, she placed it in the microwave. "This one could use a minute or so. The others are fine. Brady, what would you like to drink?"

"Water, for now."

Amanda took two bottles from the refrigerator, handing one to Brady. She looked at her mother. "Did you want to talk now or over dinner?"

"After what you and that man have done, I think it's best to talk over dinner."

"That man is Brady Blackwolf, and he's my husband. You will treat him with respect, or you'll leave." She glanced at her father, who leaned against a counter. His features remained neutral, though she spotted a flash of humor in his eyes.

The ding of the microwave halted further discussion as everyone filled plates and took them into the dining room. Amanda sat with Brady on one side of her, and Mark's father on her other side. Her father sat next to Brady, with the two women taking seats beside each other.

They ate for several minutes in silence before Mark's mother spoke. "This marriage happened rather abruptly."

Amanda shook her head. "Not really. Brady has been helping around here since before we lost Mark. Afterward, he would come by three or four times a week to help out. You do remember he was a friend of Mark's, right?"

"I vaguely recall Mark saying something about him, but it was such a long time ago," Mrs. Swanson said. "At least, it seems a long time to me. I didn't realize you and Brady spent so much time together."

"It wasn't a great deal of time until a couple months ago when Kicking Horse Ranch and Whistle Rock Ranch formed a partnership to breed and sell Morgan horses. Wyatt Bonner sent him over here full time to help out with the mares and studs the Bonner family bought to start the breeding program. We've spent a great deal of time working together after that."

"You can get the marriage annulled," Amanda's

mother blurted. "An annulment shouldn't be a problem."

Brady set down his fork, his voice hard and final. "We aren't getting the marriage annulled, Peggy."

She tried to stare him down before giving up and looking at her plate.

"Well, I don't like you remarrying so soon after Mark's death," Mrs. Swanson said. "You aren't honoring his memory very well."

Amanda felt her face heat. "He told me if anything ever happened to him, it was all right to sell the ranch and leave Brilliance. It's been two years, and I've honored him every day by continuing to work the dream we made together. I decided not to sell the ranch because of Mark, and the legacy I want to leave for Marcus." Her hands were shaking so badly, she didn't attempt to pick up her fork.

"We want you back in Vermont, Amanda. We're prepared to do whatever it takes to get you to leave this place." Her mother made a sweeping gesture with her hand.

"I don't know how you think you could force me to leave. I'm not a naïve girl of sixteen. I'm a widowed mother who has remarried a man I dearly love. Together, we are going to make this ranch a success."

"Not if I have anything to say about it," her mother huffed, glaring between her daughter and Brady. "He doesn't belong here, and neither do you."

"I'm sorry you feel that way, Mother. Brady and I are married, and our life is on this ranch. There is nothing you can do to change either of those."

Mark's father, who'd stayed silent, spoke for the first time. "Mark meant everything to us, Amanda. He was our only child, our world. His death created a hole nothing will ever be able to fill." He looked around the table. "When I hold Marcus, there is a peace I didn't believe I'd ever find again. It's as if I have Mark all over again. Amanda is the woman my son chose for his wife and to have his children. Now, Mark is gone, but Amanda and Marcus are still here, and she's staying true to his dream." His voice grew louder. "I'm not a strong man like Mark. But I refuse to take part in any action that could result in me not being able to see my grandson, Amanda...or... her new husband."

Standing, he hugged Amanda and shook Brady's hand. "Welcome to the family."

Epilogue

A few days later…

"Hey, Lucas." Tiffany jogged toward him, holding up her phone. "Call for you from the sheriff."

Straining to hear her, he reined the gelding he'd been exercising toward the fence. Tiffany held up the phone again.

"What is it?"

"The sheriff is trying to reach you. He tried your phone, then called Amanda, who called me."

Reaching out, he took it from her outstretched hand. "Sheriff?"

"You're a hard man to reach."

"I'm in a pasture with one of the horses. I left my phone inside."

"One of my deputies is moving out of state. Are you still interested in a deputy position?"

"Yes, sir, I am."

"Great. There are several requirements. I doubt you'll have any problem passing them. Stop by the station in the next couple days and pick up a packet from Cindy. I'll schedule you for the health exam, drug screen, psychological screen, and physical fitness requirement. This week good for you?"

"Yes. I'll pick up the packet later today and return what you need tomorrow. This week is fine with a day's notice. I need to square things with Amanda."

"Sounds good. I look forward to working with you, Lucas." Garth Duggan ended the call before he could respond.

"Good news?" Tiffany asked when he handed her back the phone.

"The best. There's an opening for a deputy. The sheriff called to see if I'm interested."

"And?"

"Heck, yes, I'm interested. Where's Amanda?"

"Taking Lucia back to town. She shouldn't be gone long. So this is what you came to Brilliance for?"

Dismounting, he walked the horse back into the barn. "Yeah. I could've gotten on in several cities, but this is where I want to live."

Tiffany leaned against a stall. "How'd you know Brilliance was the place?"

Setting the saddle on a rack and the tack on hooks, Lucas looked at her. "Are you thinking of staying?"

She glanced around the barn, then outside to the open pasture, wondering if this might be her special place. "Maybe."

Leading the horse into a stall, he closed the gate, then turned to face her. "Why Brilliance? Well, I came here to visit the widow of a buddy of mine."

"Oh…"

"We were tight, and I'd become good friends with her. Do you know Laurel? She owns Florals & Floats?"

"I've met her. It's a nice store."

"She's my buddy's widow. When I got here a few months ago, a deputy, Aiden Winters, had developed an interest in her. They married about a year ago. Aiden and I became friends before I had to return to California. I couldn't get this place, the people, out of my head. It may sound ridiculous, but I liked everything about this area. When I had a chance to walk away from my job, I called Sheriff Duggan and asked about becoming a deputy."

"And here you are."

He chuckled. "Yes, here I am."

"I want to find a place like this."

"I'm guessing what you want isn't in Vermont."

"Definitely not Vermont. I mean, it's a wonderful state and the people are great. I just need to get away from my parents. You've met them. Dad isn't so bad, but Mom is a bit…controlling. I don't think she's ever understood I'm an adult. Maybe moving away will help."

"I'm not sure it helped Amanda."

Chuckling, Tiffany smiled. "You're right. It might be a chronic issue with Mom. So, I'm considering a few places. I like the idea of being close to Amanda and Marcus. And now, Brady. I love horses."

"Brady told me you used to compete."

"English equestrian. Show jumping was my main

event. I'm done with all that now."

They turned at the sound of an engine and tires crunching the gravel drive.

"Sounds like Amanda may be home. I'm going to let her know I have to drive to town."

Tiffany nodded. "Sure."

Her gaze followed him until he left the barn, her thoughts on what he'd said about Brilliance. She did like it here. Everything about it appealed to her. And there was something else attractive about Brilliance.

It would soon be home to one of the town's finest. Lucas Kovak.

Learn about upcoming books in **The Cowboys of Whistle Rock Ranch** series at shirleendavies.com.

Enjoy the Whistle Rock Cowboys? You might want to read **Macklins of Whiskey Bend**.

If you want to keep current on all my preorders, new releases, and other happenings, sign up for my newsletter at **shirleendavies.com/contact**.

A Note from Shirleen

Thank you for reading **The Cowboy's Simple Solution**!

Leave a Review! If you enjoyed the, please consider posting a short review and telling your friends. Word of mouth is an author's best friend and is much appreciated.

I care about quality, so if you find something in error, please contact me via email at **shirleen@shirleendavies.com**.

Books by Shirleen Davies

Contemporary Western Romance Series

Macklins of Whiskey Bend

Thorn
Del
Boone
Kell
Zane

Cowboy's of Whistle Rock Ranch

The Cowboy's Road Home, Book One
The Cowboy's False Start, Book Two
The Cowboy's Second Chance Family, Book Three
The Cowboy's Final Ride, Book Four
The Cowboy's Surprise Reunion, Book Five
The Cowboy's Counterfeit Fiancée, Book Six
The Cowboy's Ultimate Challenge, Book Seven
The Cowboy's Simple Solution, Book Eight
The Cowboy's Broken Dream, Book Nine, Coming
Next in the Series!

MacLarens of Fire Mountain

Second Summer, Book One
Hard Landing, Book Two

One More Day, Book Three
All Your Nights, Book Four
Always Love You, Book Five
Hearts Don't Lie, Book Six
No Getting Over You, Book Seven
'Til the Sun Comes Up, Book Eight
Foolish Heart, Book Nine

Historical Western Romance Series

Redemption Mountain

Redemption's Edge, Book One
Wildfire Creek, Book Two
Sunrise Ridge, Book Three
Dixie Moon, Book Four
Survivor Pass, Book Five
Promise Trail, Book Six
Deep River, Book Seven
Courage Canyon, Book Eight
Forsaken Falls, Book Nine
Solitude Gorge, Book Ten
Rogue Rapids, Book Eleven
Angel Peak, Book Twelve
Restless Wind, Book Thirteen
Storm Summit, Book Fourteen
Mystery Mesa, Book Fifteen
Thunder Valley, Book Sixteen
A Very Splendor Christmas, Holiday Novella, Book
Seventeen

Paradise Point, Book Eighteen
Silent Sunset, Book Nineteen
Rocky Basin, Book Twenty
Captive Dawn, Book Twenty-One
Whisper Lake, Another Very Splendor Christmas,
Book Twenty-Two
Mustang Meadow, Book Twenty-Three
Solitary Glen, Book Twenty-Four
Ghost Lagoon, Book Twenty-Five
Renegade Woods, Book Twenty-Six, Coming Next in
the Series!

MacLarens of Fire Mountain

Tougher than the Rest, Book One
Faster than the Rest, Book Two
Harder than the Rest, Book Three
Stronger than the Rest, Book Four
Deadlier than the Rest, Book Five
Wilder than the Rest, Book Six

MacLarens of Boundary Mountain

Colin's Quest, Book One,
Brodie's Gamble, Book Two
Quinn's Honor, Book Three
Sam's Legacy, Book Four
Heather's Choice, Book Five
Nate's Destiny, Book Six
Blaine's Wager, Book Seven
Fletcher's Pride, Book Eight
Bay's Desire, Book Nine
Cam's Hope, Book Ten

Romantic Suspense

Eternal Brethren Military Romantic Suspense

Steadfast, Book One
Shattered, Book Two
Haunted, Book Three
Untamed, Book Four
Devoted, Book Five
Faithful, Book Six
Exposed, Book Seven
Undaunted, Book Eight
Resolute, Book Nine
Unspoken, Book Ten
Defiant, Book Eleven

Peregrine Bay Romantic Suspense

Reclaiming Love, Book One
Our Kind of Love, Book Two

Find all of my books at: shirleendavies.com

About Shirleen

Shirleen Davies writes romance—historical and contemporary western romance, and romantic suspense. She grew up in Southern California, attended Oregon State University, and has degrees from San Diego State University and the University of Maryland. During the day she provides consulting services to small and mid-sized businesses. But her real passion is writing emotionally charged stories of flawed people who find redemption through love and acceptance. She now lives with her husband in a beautiful town in northern Arizona.

I love to hear from my readers!
Send me an email: shirleen@shirleendavies.com
Visit my Website: www.shirleendavies.com
Sign up to be notified of New Releases:
www.shirleendavies.com/contact
Follow me on Amazon:
amazon.com/author/shirleendavies
Follow me on BookBub:
bookbub.com/authors/shirleen-davies

Other ways to connect with me:
Facebook Author Page:
facebook.com/shirleendaviesauthor
Pinterest: pinterest.com/shirleendavies
Instagram: instagram.com/shirleendavies_author
TikTok: shirleendavies_author
Twitter: www.twitter.com/shirleendavies